A BOOKSHOP TO DIE FOR

A WONDERLAND BOOKS MYSTERY

BOOK ONE

M.P. BLACK

For A & L—all for one, and one for all.

CHAPTER 1

*A*lice Hartford stepped into Blithedale Books, gripping her silver-sequined clutch in one hand and the train of her white wedding dress in the other.

Behind the counter stood a pasty-faced man in his fifties. When he caught sight of Alice, he scowled.

"We don't do weddings," he grumbled.

"I'm looking for something…"

"A groom?" The man snorted at his own joke, though he seemed incapable of smiling, his mouth constantly turning down in a fish-like frown.

Alice didn't laugh. She was barely able to hold back her tears.

"A book. I'm looking for a book."

She had no desire to tell this man the truth. She wanted to be left alone in her special place. Her hideaway. She only hoped it was still there.

"Books I've got," the man grumbled, and he waved dismissively at the bookshelves that dominated the store. "But don't expect a pity discount."

Alice scanned the bookstore. It was nothing like she remembered.

Long ago, when her mom had run the little bookshop, it had been cozy and welcoming, decorated with posters of famous covers. Bean bag chairs for readers to sit in. Colorful cardboard mobiles dangling on thin wires from the ceiling—ladies in frilly dresses, fire-breathing dragons, rocket ships, all turning slowly in the breeze from the open windows.

But the bookstore she moved across now bore no signs of that happy past.

The rows of bookshelves sagged. Below her pearl-lined wedding flats, the linoleum floor looked shabby. Tiles had come undone, exposing bare concrete.

What did she expect? That Blithedale Books hadn't changed over the past twenty years? She'd been nine years old when her mom got the diagnosis—a death sentence, really—and the bookstore had been sold. A year later, her mom was cremated, her ashes scattered on her favorite beach, and Alice moved in with her pleasant but somewhat indifferent aunt and uncle.

All these years, she thought sadly, *and I wait to come back now. When it's probably too late.*

She approached one of the shelves and pretended to browse, aware that the owner was watching her with interest.

It was impossible to look inconspicuous in a wedding dress. Yesterday, Sunday, she'd missed the last bus to Blithedale, slept on a bench at the station, and then caught the first departure in the morning. On the bus to Blithedale, she'd stood out like a sore thumb. Arriving in town at noon, she'd felt even more conspicuous—in the city people weren't easily surprised, but a wayward bride appearing on Main Street in the middle of an ordinary Monday turned a lot of heads.

At least as she moved deeper into the stacks, she'd be alone. The owner would lose sight of her, and there were no other customers in the store. The only other person was a handyman. He stood on scaffolding at the very back, crouching slightly under the ceiling as he tapped at the brick wall with a hammer and chisel.

She continued to peruse the books.

Many paperbacks on the shelves had yellowed and warped. None of the spines had that glossy, promising look of a new world worth entering. She spotted classics as well as bestsellers from a couple of decades ago. Had this guy even restocked since buying the bookstore from her mom? If so, he seemed to have put in repeat orders, relying on her mom's sense of what was worth stocking. And sold few copies over the years.

Could this mean that Alice would find her old favorites on the shelves?

She looked through the Cs. Cervantes. Chesterton. Christie. But no Carroll, the author she was looking for.

She moved down the aisle between the bookshelves, her dress sweeping up dirt behind her. She didn't care. After bolting down the church aisle, she hadn't stopped running until she'd reached the bus station. That was a mile of city grime she'd swept up. Even after the bus dropped her off in Blithedale, she'd only held up the train to keep from tripping. The dress was ruined.

Rich would be shocked. But then he had other things to worry about right now—like his bride leaving him at the altar.

She fiddled with her engagement ring, turning it. It fit perfectly. Yet it felt too tight.

She pushed her thoughts aside. None of that mattered right now. What mattered was whether, after twenty years, the red door was still there.

Her clutch buzzed, as if she'd trapped a colony of bees inside. That would be Rich calling her for the 100th time. She ignored him.

Twenty years had passed, she reminded herself as she came to the end of the row of shelves without finding anything. Any sign of her mom's creativity, her love for books, and the joy she got from sharing that love was gone. Of course the red door would be gone too.

At the back of the store, she reached the scaffolding. She turned left, continuing her search. She turned yet another corner among the stacks. And came to a standstill.

Her hands tingled. No bookshelves stood along the brick wall. Instead, boxes stood heaped in a makeshift stack. She crept closer. In a crack between the boxes, something red caught her eye.

Is that it...?

She reached out to pull the boxes aside, when someone spoke behind her.

"You are either very engaged," the man said, "or very single."

CHAPTER 2

A man stood in the aisle, hands on his hips. Long hair in a pony tail. Cargo shorts with a tool belt. Tank top.

He grinned. "It's not every day we get a runaway bride in Blithedale."

Was it her imagination or did he puff up his chest to show her his well-defined pecs?

Alice took a step away from the boxes, hoping her behavior didn't look as suspicious as it felt.

But if the handyman suspected anything, he didn't show it. He was too busy studying her. No, not studying her. He was gazing at her, as if she were a wedding cake and he was trying to guess what filling was inside. Gross.

"I'm Vince. And hey, once I finish fixing this leak in the roof—" He stuck out a thumb, gesturing at the scaffolding that rose to the ceiling at the back. "—I'll be happy to show you around town. Don't tell me you have plans."

Just then, the pasty-faced owner rounded the corner, rescuing her. He scowled at Vince and said, "Mr. Malone.

Miss Cox and I are going to the diner for a business meeting. I'll be back soon."

"Take your time, Bunce," Vince said. "I'll keep an eye on —" He paused. "—things."

A woman joined them. She wore a navy blazer, a white button-down, and a gold watch with matching bracelet and necklace that made her look so much more professional and adult than either Bunce or Vince. Apparently, Vince wasn't impressed. He winked at her. But her attention was already drawn to Alice, her eyes widening.

"Sweetheart, what happened to you?"

She rushed forward and grabbed one of Alice's hands.

"No gentlemen left in the world," the woman muttered, and set about brushing off Alice's dress.

"Oh, don't bother," Alice said. "It's ruined anyway. But thanks for your help."

"I'm Kristin Cox, realtor, but everyone calls me Kris."

"I don't," Bunce said.

"And that's fine, Bunce." With her back to Bunce, Kris rolled her eyes at Alice, and Alice couldn't help but smile. Kris said, "We're headed to the diner to meet with a couple, Mr. and Mrs. Oriel. They want to buy the bookstore."

The words squeezed Alice's heart. "Buy the bookstore?"

She'd come all this way to make sure the bookstore, with all its happy memories, continued to live on. And it was going to be sold?

Kris nudged Alice playfully. "Hey, want to buy a bookstore? It's a great deal. Imagine owning your own bookstore in this quaint little town."

"I could never…" Alice muttered, trying to imagine what it would be like to start a new life in Blithedale. Her old life lay in ruins. No apartment. That had been Rich's. No job. Rich had not only been her fiancé, but also her boss at his independent bookstore in the city. And no real friends. Her uncle had been in the army, and they'd moved around a lot. Every year, she got invited to three different high school reunions. She had acquaintances in a dozen states, lots of friends on social media, and no one to confide in.

Years ago, her aunt and uncle had retired to Costa Rica. Apart from Christmas and birthday cards, Alice didn't communicate with them. They had even declined the invitation to the wedding, saying Alice surely understood that, at their age, such a long trip was out of the question. Alice understood, or said she did.

"No better place than Blithedale," Kris said, and squeezed Alice's arm, a sympathetic gesture that made her chest tighten. "I can drive you around town and I guarantee you'll fall in love. Maybe you really will want to bid on the bookstore."

Bunce cut in. "We already have buyers, Miss Cox."

"I would if I could," Alice mumbled. "Who are these buyers? What are they going to do with the bookstore?"

"Fix it up," Kris said. "They love the idea of an oasis for book lovers."

Alice let out a breath, relieved to hear it. After realizing she wasn't happy with Rich, the thing she needed most in her life was to make sure the sliver of her old self that remained —her happy childhood at the bookstore—would somehow be preserved. If these buyers genuinely wanted to revitalize Blithedale Books, she could talk to them about saving her hideaway—and ensuring the happy memories from her childhood lived on.

"Whether you're interested or not," Kris added, interrupting her thoughts, "we can show you where most of Blithedale hangs out: the What the Dickens Diner."

"Thanks," Alice said. "But I'm looking for—" She paused. "—a book."

Bunce said, "You can let yourself out, then. But don't

think you're not being watched. I have security cameras. Thieves will be prosecuted."

Kris sighed and treated Alice to another eye-roll. "Nobody believes you're a thief. Besides, Bunce is too cheap to pay for security. Just watch out for that guy Vince. He's trouble."

A moment later, the front door banged shut.

Alice was left alone in the bookstore with Vince. The handyman was back on his perch on top of the scaffolding, thwacking a hammer against something in the wall. He seemed to have lost interest in anything but his work.

She grabbed the first box and pulled it out. Then removed another. And yet another. Soon, she had cleared enough of the boxes to see what lay behind. Butterflies flurried in her stomach. Tears welled in her eyes.

Behind the boxes stood an antique wardrobe. It had a single, narrow door, the paint flaking off. In spite of the toll that the years had taken, this was easily recognizable: the red door from her childhood.

She stepped up to it, her heart racing. She almost didn't dare touch it, in case it would vanish, proving to be a figment of her overactive imagination.

A hand-painted sign on the door said, "DO NOT ENTER," a sign she herself had made.

She put a hand on the door. Flakes of paint came loose and fluttered to the linoleum, like fall leaves. She grasped the little metal knob and pulled. The hinges creaked. The door swung open.

CHAPTER 3

*A*lice let out a little sob that was half a laugh.

The wardrobe looked the same as she remembered. Or almost the same, anyway. There were cushions piled up in the little space. A nook with little shelves held books. Nancy Drew. C.S. Lewis's Narnia books. Lois Lowry's *Number the Stars.*

Her mom, running a bookstore and raising a kid, had found a creative way to keep Alice busy the many hours she spent at Blithedale Books.

"This is your magical hideaway," her mom had told her. "Your Wonderland. No one else gets to come in, unless you invite them. Only people you love—and who love you."

"Then you can come in, Mommy," Alice had said.

Her mom laughed and touched Alice's face. "I will, Sweetpea. If I can fit."

Now her mom's comment made sense as Alice wedged herself through the narrow opening. She eased herself down onto the cushions, and only got halfway before the awkwardness of the dress overturned her and she dumped down on her butt.

She let out an "Oomph!"

But at least she was sitting down.

Cobwebs tangled in her hair and she brushed them away.

The space was much smaller than it had once been—or rather she was bigger. The giant dress didn't help. Her legs extended beyond the door, and it would be difficult to close it.

But dammit, she'd come all this way and she wasn't about to give up.

She raised one leg, twisting it, so she could shove it into the wardrobe, knee up against one wall. One of the bookshelves dug into her back. The other leg came next. She tried to retract it. But she wasn't a turtle. Instead, she had to bend it and grab it with both hands and yank it toward her butt. Gently, she closed the door, until she heard the beloved snick of the latch closing.

Her legs ached. The edge of the shelf behind her stabbed her back. Something under the cushion—something hard—poked at her thigh. But at least she was inside.

She let out a long sigh. She'd found her hideaway again, the last place she'd truly felt like she knew herself. After her mom's diagnosis, it was as if the world cracked, and nothing quite looked right again. With every move across the country, more cracks showed in the glass, and Alice receded deeper and deeper into herself and her books.

She breathed in—and coughed. It was dusty in the hideaway. And cobwebs filled the corners. But as she closed her eyes, she imagined what it had felt like to sit in this place and know that her mom was behind the counter, selling books. For a moment, she felt it. She could taste the chocolate chip cookies her mom brought her, the cold milk, the sound of the cash register ring-dinging as her mom made another sale. The chatter of happy customers.

"My love for you will live on forever," she heard her mom

say. "You'll find it where and when you need it the most."

Alice wiped a hand across her face. It was wet with tears. She shifted her position.

Ouch.

There really wasn't much room in this wardrobe. And this hard thing under the cushion wasn't making things better.

She shoved a hand underneath and found the object and pulled it out.

It was a book.

She gasped. It wasn't just any book. It was the one she'd been looking for.

Lewis Carroll's *Alice's Adventures in Wonderland.*

Could it really be the case that this book, which she'd hid twenty years ago under a cushion, had been left undisturbed all these years for her to find again? What were the chances?

She opened to page 1 and read the first line:

Alice was beginning to get very tired of sitting by her sister on the bank, and of having nothing to do: once or twice she had peeped into the book her sister was reading, but it had no pictures or conversations in it, "and what is the use of a book," thought Alice "without pictures or conversations?"

And as she read the familiar lines, she could almost hear her mom reading them to her at night as a small child. Snuggled close to Mommy. Her soft, warm body against her. Still so alive with love.

Something hot rose in her throat, choking her. Then a sob broke through. Then another. The tears trickled down, and there was nothing she could do—or wanted to do—to stop them.

She gripped the book, pressing it to her chest, and wept, and wept, and wept.

CHAPTER 4

*A*lice woke to a sharp pain in her back and one leg, which was pressed awkwardly against the door. She didn't mind. With the door shut, she was enjoying the privacy of her hideaway. If Vince came snooping or Bunce returned—or even if the friendly Kris came looking—she hoped they'd assume she'd left the bookstore.

A weight had lifted from her shoulders. The crying had done her good. For the first time in years, she felt more like herself.

She was reading about the other Alice talking to the caterpillar, and it was as if Lewis Carroll had written a secret message just for her:

"Who are you?" said the Caterpillar.

This was not an encouraging opening for a conversation. Alice replied, rather shyly, "I—I hardly know, sir, just at present—at least I know who I was when I got up this morning, but I think I must have been changed several times since then."

"What do you mean by that?" said the Caterpillar sternly. "Explain yourself!"

"I can't explain myself, I'm afraid, sir," said Alice, "because I'm not myself, you see."

She was considering the deeper meaning of this, when she heard a scream and a crash.

The ruckus made her jump. Only she had no room to jump, so instead she kicked out and the little red door flew open with a bang.

Footsteps slapped against the linoleum. A person ran down the aisle at breakneck speed. A pair of legs whizzed past, shoes slap-slapping on the linoleum.

"Hey," Alice called out. "What's going on?"

She struggled with her dress, scrambling to get up. She'd had none of the advantages of a turtle retracting its limbs when she sat down, yet here she was feeling like she was stuck on her back, her legs and arms flailing to turn herself over. She cursed.

Finally, she managed to free her twisted left leg and inch her butt across the cushions and then dump out into the bookstore aisle.

She landed on her hands and knees. She got to her feet and, out of habit, brushed down her dress. Then stopped.

What was that crash she'd heard?

She looked around. Bookshelves stretched out in either direction. Overhead, she could make out the scaffolding near the ceiling, but no handyman.

She gazed back at her hideaway. Reluctant to leave it so soon, she nevertheless slipped the book under the cushion and closed the red door again.

She retraced her steps to the front. Bunce had not returned yet. A sheet of paper taped to the cash register carried a hastily scribbled message in a rough hand:

Be back in 5 minutes. Thieves will be prosecuted!!!

She went looking for Vince. She headed straight down one of the aisles. Only there was no straight line to the back. The bookshelves had been arranged at angles, creating a kind of labyrinth.

Her mom had arranged the bookshelves in such a way. "A bookstore holds treasures that look different to every person," her mom had said. "What you find, won't be what I find, because the magic will make sure you find precisely what you need."

Bunce's neglect had turned that whimsical idea into something far more mundane: The bookstore felt like a chaotic mess.

She rounded a corner and, although the scaffolding lay to the left, labyrinth logic told her to turn right at the next intersection. She turned right, then left, and headed down a straight stretch until she emerged at the end of the stacks.

The scaffolding rose above her, and she called out Vince's name.

Then she saw him, and stopped.

Vince lay on the floor, face down, blood pooling under his head.

Her stomach leaped up her throat. She put a hand to her mouth, stifling a scream.

He must have fallen. She crouched down over him.

"Vince?"

She put a hand on his back. He wasn't moving. She put two fingers to his neck to feel for a pulse. Nothing. Then his wrist. Also nothing.

Alice's heart raced. A horrible accident. Vince was dead.

But then she remembered the person running past the red door, and a cold hand gripped her heart. If Vince fell by accident, why would that someone run away?

CHAPTER 5

*A*lice's sequined clutch buzzed on the formica tabletop, and everyone around the table stared at it.

A couple of hours had passed since she'd discovered Vince's body, and Chief of Police James Sapling, Jr. had gathered Alice, Bunce, and Kris in a booth at the local diner. As Kris had mentioned, the place was called What the Dickens Diner, and on the walls hung framed illustrations from Charles Dickens' books. The one by their booth was of Oliver Twist asking for another serving of gruel.

The baby-faced chief of police and Bunce sat on one side, with Kris and Alice on the other.

All four stared at the clutch, waiting for the buzzing to stop.

Finally, silence.

"Let's begin," the chief of police said.

Alice's knowledge of police procedure came mostly from books and episodes of *Law & Order*, but she was pretty sure this wasn't the right way to do a police interview.

"Shouldn't you be questioning us individually, Chief Sapling?"

"Jimbo."

Alice wasn't sure what that meant. As the chief of police checked a little book he had by his side and scribbled on a notepad, she looked to Kris and Bunce for help.

Across the formica table, Bunce was busy perfecting his frown. Kris, who sat next to Alice, whispered, "He prefers Jimbo. Chief Jimbo. Chief Sapling was what everyone called his dad."

His dad? Did this mean that the role of police chief was handed down from father to son in Blithedale?

And what was that book the chief of police consulted every two minutes? He closed it and Alice got a glimpse of the cover: *The Police Chief Companion: 21 Days to Killing It On the Job.*

Her first impression—that Chief Jimbo wasn't your usual, stereotypical gray-haired chief of police, and that it was nice to see a younger man in the job—suddenly took on new meaning. He was an inexperienced kid.

"Nothing in the book about that," he said. "Besides, Miss Hartford, this is a single cop town. We have to be efficient. Nobody's got any secrets here, especially not in a simple case like this."

"Look, I saw someone," Alice said. "I saw—"

Chief Jimbo held up a hand and smiled. "Hold on. We may be efficient, but we also have to wait our turn. That's only polite."

He glanced from person to person, and finally settled on Bunce. "Mr. Bunce, why don't you tell me what happened?"

Bunce proceeded to complain about how he'd had to deal with Vince that morning as well as a whole string of menial tasks. "Owning that business has been a curse from day one. Twenty years of torture. And now this. I'll be glad to sell the damn place to the Oriels and finally retire."

He explained how Kris had come to the bookstore to

17

fetch him for a meeting at the diner with a couple named Mr. and Mrs. Oriel who were interested in buying the bookstore. Alice remembered that Kris had mentioned them.

"And you met this young lady, too," Chief Jimbo said. He was far too young to refer to Alice as *young lady*.

Just then Alice's phone rang again, her clutch buzzing.

"I did," Bunce said and gave Alice a disapproving look. "But she stayed at the bookstore while Kris and I came over here."

"So you didn't see Vince's accident?"

Bunce shook his head.

Next Chief Jimbo asked Kris to recount what she'd seen. Her story matched Bunce's perfectly, only she added a bit more detail about first meeting Alice, sharing how worried she'd been to see a woman in a wedding dress, obviously in a state of distress. She turned to Alice. "I should've stayed and made sure you were all right. Maybe if I hadn't been so busy with the sale, this tragedy wouldn't have happened."

"Which brings us to you, Miss Hartford."

"I arrived at the bookstore around noon," she said.

"And where were you coming from?"

"From the city."

"Can you be more specific?"

"From church."

Chief Jimbo blinked. Then stared down at his notepad, his cheeks turning red. Alice noticed that he wore no ring. "Guess we don't need more details on that," he mumbled. Then said, "All right, tell me what happened in the bookstore."

Alice proceeded to summarize what had happened, though she simply said that she'd sat down in a reading nook to read, leaving out the details about the red door and her hideaway and the connection she felt to Blithedale Books.

She had no desire to share her story—that was between her and her mom.

"Then I heard a loud crash. It startled me. I accidentally kicked open the door."

Chief Jimbo raised his eyebrows. "The door to the bookstore?"

Alice hesitated. "I mean, I kicked out, startled. And nearly tripped someone. They ran past me."

"Who was it?"

"I didn't see."

Chief Jimbo wrote something on his notepad, ending his scrawl with a flurry.

"Well, thank you all for your testimonies. You've been so helpful." He smiled at them all, getting a smile back from Kris and a sour frown from Bunce. "I'll be in touch if I need anything from you. Miss Hartford, do you have an address I can reach you at? Or a phone number?"

He stared at the sequined clutch on the table. They all were. It was buzzing again.

"I'll be staying at a hotel," Alice said. "And here's my number."

She rattled off the numbers. Then added, as she continued to ignore her phone's insistent buzzing, "Although, if you need me urgently, maybe call the hotel. I don't always answer my phone. Except, I don't know which hotel I'm staying a yet."

Chief Jimbo smiled. "Pemberley Inn. It's the only one in town."

He scooted out of the booth, gathering up his book and notepad. In the process, he knocked over a coffee cup. The black liquid sloshed onto his pants.

"Oh, shoot."

He grabbed a napkin and dabbed at it. His uniform, Alice

noted, already had a long yellow streak down the front. A mustard stain, no doubt.

"When will you know more about what happened at the bookstore?" she asked.

For a moment, he looked confused. He balled up the napkin and tossed it on the table. He opened his book, flipped through the pages, and said, "Well, first, we secure the scene and document everything. That's done. Then we notify the coroner. Also done. Interviewing witnesses. Done. So, really, there's just preparing the report. Then there'll be a funeral and we can all—" He gazed off in the distance, a sailor who's relieved to see land. "—move on with our lives."

CHAPTER 6

"You look like someone who needs a strong cup of coffee. And something to eat."

The woman in the apron smiled, revealing a gap between her front teeth. She was both tall and wide and her big, curly black hair added to her already considerable bulk. Her apron said, "What the Dickens Diner—for the best of times and the worst of times."

"Milk?" she asked as she held out a coffee pot. "Sugar?"

Alice shook her head. So, after giving Kris and Mr. Bunce a refill, the woman topped up Alice's cup too.

She cocked her head. "You know, you look so much like someone I ought to know. Have we met before?"

Alice stared down at her coffee cup, trying to hide her emotion. She was exhausted. She wished she could curl up in her hideaway—her Wonderland—and not have to talk to anyone. And the last thing she wanted to do was talk about her personal connection to Blithedale.

"I'm sorry for prying," the woman said. "Let me get you some food. It won't be much, since I've got half the town in the diner and my one waitress off duty. I'm Becca Frye, by the way. This is my diner. I'm sorry about your trouble."

Alice thanked Becca and said, "Thanks for saying so—it was pretty awful to find Vince."

"Oh, sure, that too. But I meant about losing your fiancé."

"I didn't exactly lose him…" Alice took a sip of coffee and tried to hide her discomfort. "Besides, what bothers me is that I found Vince's body and saw someone run out of the bookstore. Though no one seems to believe me."

"Oh, I'm sure everyone believes you," Becca said.

"I don't," Bunce said.

"Well, I do. It's just that a shock like that…"

She shook her head, and Alice understood that she didn't mean the shock of finding a dead man, but rather the shock of her wedding falling apart.

"All I'm saying is that you must be exhausted."

There was no denying Becca's statement. Alice's arms and legs ached. Pain radiated up from her lower back to the top of her spine, gripping her neck. Her head throbbed. She closed her eyes for a moment.

"Clearly hysterical," Bunce said. "Imagining things."

Alice opened her eyes again. Her aching tiredness flared into anger. "Look, I did see someone. I didn't hallucinate or imagine it."

"Anyway," Becca said, changing the topic, "I know what everyone will say about Vince's death."

"They're all idiots," Bunce said.

"Oh, now, Bunce, be nice."

"They read that tabloid and they believe its lies and then I have to deal with it."

"*The Blithedale Record*," Kris explained to Alice. "It's our local paper. Entirely online. And it's run by Todd Townsend, who handles all the town news."

"News," Bunce scoffed. "You can hardly call it *news*."

Kris brought out her phone and, opening a browser, showed Alice a news site. The top headline said, "Tragic accident at deathtrap bookstore."

"Wow, there's already a story on Vince's death," Alice said, as Kris retrieved her phone. "There's even a quote by Chief Jimbo about the status of the investigation."

"News travels fast in Blithedale," Becca said. She jabbed a thumb over her shoulder. "Todd is sitting in a booth over there typing away on his laptop right now."

Alice leaned out of the booth. Across the diner, a tall, gangly man sat hunched over a laptop in a booth tapping at the keys.

But her view got cut off when a man stepped in front of her. She was staring at his gut. She looked up. He wasn't tall —certainly under 6 feet—though from her current vantage point, he towered over her. Plus, he had a squareness to him that made him imposing. The dark blue suit with a crimson tie added gravitas.

"You must be the young lady," he said with a smile, "who's lost her fiancé."

"Woman," she corrected him. "And I'm the one who found Vince's body."

Where did that come from?

She was surprised by her own pluck. Her mom had taught her to stand up for herself, but that side of her had been muffled for so long—in part, because of Rich's influence.

The man offered his hand, unperturbed by her correction. "Darrell Townsend. Welcome to Blithedale."

She shook it. "Townsend?"

As if the name was a magic word, the tall, gangly guy whom Becca had identified as a journalist materialized at

23

Darrell Townsend's side, notepad in hand. In spite of one being tall and the other broad, their faces looked like variations on the same theme. There was no doubt about them being brothers.

"Are you the mayor?" she asked Darrell.

He flashed a big smile. His teeth were so sparkling clean, you might have used them as a makeup mirror.

"Oh no, Mayor MacDonald has that honor. I'm merely a humble citizen. And the owner of Townsend Development, the area's premier real estate development company. But I prefer to think of us as a *rejuvenation engine*."

"Fancy words," Bunce grumbled, "for bulldozers and concrete."

"My interest is in the future of this town," Darrell said, ignoring Bunce. "And a tragic death, like the one today, is a blight on Blithedale's name."

"Good one," Todd Townsend muttered, hunched over his notepad, pencil scratching on paper. "Blight. Blithedale."

"Which is why," Darrell continued, his voice rising, as if he were speaking to a larger audience than just this diner booth, "I personally appreciate you cooperating with local law enforcement."

"Well, you're welcome," Alice said, confused by the theatrics. "I don't think Vince's death was an accident. But except for Becca, people don't believe me."

"Oh, I believe you."

"You do?"

"In fact, I believe we all know who the killer is."

"Really?"

This was something. Would she actually witness Darrell Townsend point to the killer right here in the local diner?

"Who?" she asked.

"A killer who's been waiting to strike," he said, swiveling

around to address the entire diner. He raised his voice. "A killer we all turned a blind eye to…" He paused for effect, apparently confident he had everyone's attention.

Darrell raised a hand, turned on Bunce, and pointed. "Blithedale Books killed Vince Malone."

CHAPTER 7

"*W*ait, what?"

Alice turned to Kris and Bunce for help, but both were frowning, staring up at Darrell Townsend.

"How can a bookstore be a killer?"

Todd Townsend shushed her. Alice looked around and saw, to her surprise, that Darrell had a rapt audience. Becca perched on the seat that Chief Jimbo had recently vacated. Up at the counter, two men in matching caps and vests and lumberjack shirts had turned their stools to face Darrell, one whispering to the other, who nodded. At a nearby table, a father nudged one of his kids, chiding him for not listening. A trio of white-haired women in a booth, a game of cards laid out on the formica tabletop, had paused their activity, and one of them was filming Darrell's speech with her smartphone.

"Today, I attended the fifth annual Pantheon of World Real Estate & Development, one of the industry's most prestigious events," Darrell said. "The organizers saw fit to award me, Darrell Townsend, a prize for the most visionary small-town real estate development plan. But awards and prizes and other such accolades mean little to me." He swept a hand through the air, dismissing them all. "I have a wall full of them. In fact, at first I turned down their invitation. Why waste half a workday on a prize ceremony? Why add another trophy to my wall? But then I realized that this wasn't for me. It was for Blithedale. And this town deserves all the awards it gets."

Todd Townsend put his pencil behind his ear and his notepad under his arm and applauded, glaring at everyone, urging them to join in.

"Thank you, friends," Darrell said. "So that's why I went to the city. I went because we live in what's probably the best town in America."

More applause, led by Todd.

Darrell held up a hand to stop the clapping. "Hold your horses. Did you catch that? I said *probably*. I don't know about you, but I don't want to live in what's *probably* or *perhaps* or even *likely* the best. Who wants to wake up in the morning in what's *probably* the best town? Not me. Heck, I'll settle for nothing less than hands down the best. Numero uno. And I know that's how you feel, too. "

He looked around, nodding, his face serious.

"But folks, we've got problems in this town. Setbacks that bring us down to *probably* and *perhaps*, and if nothing's done, Blithedale will fall farther down the ranking. I'm talking about places like Blithedale Books. When was the last time any of you set foot in that place?"

Most people shrugged or shook their heads.

"Well, I've taken a look around, and let me tell you, it ain't pretty. That place is falling apart. I've said before, and I'll say it again, Blithedale Books is a safety concern and ought to be shut down. I warned everyone. So did Todd here. You read the articles in *The Blithedale Record*, and you probably thought we were exaggerating. Now a man's dead."

He lowered his head, acknowledging the tragic event.

But not for long. He jerked his attention back up to his audience, gazing intently at the people scattered across the diner.

He said, "It's not my job to decide what happens to that death trap. I leave that to Mayor MacDonald and Chief Jimbo. But I'm happy to recommend an independent building inspector to take a close look at the structure, and make sure no other tragic deaths happen."

He ended with a smile and a wave, and his hand stayed suspended in the air just long enough for his brother to circle him and snap several photos with his phone. Then he turned around and gestured at Chief Jimbo, who was standing at the far end of the diner counter, and the young chief of police stiffened.

"Jimbo." Darrell walked over and put an arm around Chief Jimbo's shoulders. "Let's talk."

CHAPTER 8

"That snake," Bunce hissed. His pasty complexion had turned purple. "Darrell's only trying to force a sale at the lowest price, so he can snap up the property himself. If it weren't for Mr. and Mrs. Oriel, who are signing the papers in a few days, Darrell would sink his teeth into it."

"But a week ago, before the Oriels showed up, you were going to sell to Darrell," Kris said.

"I'd rather the ceiling collapsed on me than sell to that viper."

Having seen the state of the bookstore, Alice wondered whether Bunce meant that literally. "What does all this mean? What will happen to the bookstore?"

"Don't worry," Kris said. "The Oriels will do a great job of running the bookstore."

"Better than Darrell Townsend," Becca agreed, and Alice was surprised to see her screw up her nose, as if she smelled something nasty. Apparently not everyone loved Darrell Townsend.

"What is this visionary plan he has for Blithedale?" Alice asked. "What would he do if he got the bookstore?"

"Knock it down and build a parking lot," Becca said. "Blithedale doesn't even need a parking lot, but it's all part of Darrell's vision. First the parking lot. Then the strip malls, fast food restaurants, and big box stores."

"Build a parking lot? But can he even do that?"

"He already got permission from Mayor MacDonald." Becca leaned closer to Alice, lowering her voice conspiratorially. "Some of us suspect the mayor's been promised exclusivity on the properties Darrell plans to build and sell."

"Those are rumors," Kris said, but her protest sounded weak, and when Alice looked at her, she stared down at her cup of coffee.

"Listen up," someone called out from across the diner. It was Todd Townsend, getting everyone's attention.

Alice leaned out of the booth. Down at the end of the counter, Darrell and Todd Townsend stood on either side of Chief Jimbo. Darrell slapped Jimbo on the back and grinned. Jimbo nodded eagerly, and Alice couldn't help but think of a puppy wagging its tail. Even at this distance, she could hear Darrell say, "Go ahead, Jimbo, tell them."

Chief Jimbo slipped off his stool. Holding his police chief manual in his hands, wringing the paperback nervously, he spoke. Only his voice was so low, Alice couldn't hear a word.

"Speak up, Jimbo," one of the men at the counter said. "You can do it, buddy."

A smile on Chief Jimbo's face flickered and faltered, and he tugged at the collar of his shirt.

"As I was saying…"

He cleared his throat. Todd Townsend gave him a shove, which sent him stumbling forward. A few people chuckled.

"Clumsy me," Chief Jimbo said, and then pretended to stumble again. That got a laugh from a few people, which seemed to give him confidence.

My God, Alice thought. *He's the class clown.*

A range of emotions ran through her: horror, frustration, but also deep sympathy for a man who was clearly not the master of his own destiny.

"I, uh. I want to make an announcement," Chief Jimbo said. "Pending the investigation into Blithedale Books, uh—" He glanced back at Darrell, who gave him a nod. "—and its safety and structural integrity—" Checking with Darrell again. "—the bookstore will be closed to the public."

Alice gasped. It was as if someone had punched her in the gut.

"No, he can't," she said.

Becca sighed and shook her head. "He just did. He just did."

CHAPTER 9

*A*fter Darrell's performance, Bunce returned to the bookstore, escorted by Chief Jimbo to ensure he locked up the business.

Becca excused herself. "I've got one waitress, Susan Malone. That's Vince's widow. I naturally sent her home to grieve. But that means I've got to hustle."

That left Alice and Kris in the booth.

Kris checked her watch.

"Mr. and Mrs. Oriel will be here any minute. We're taking a look at a house they may want to buy." She glanced at Alice. "Are you okay?"

Alice shook her head. "I can't believe it. I've just gotten here, and found the bookstore, and now it's closed."

"Don't worry. Darrell hasn't won. Chief Jimbo can close the bookstore for 48 hours, but then he'll need evidence that there's a problem with the store, or he'll need to get a court order to keep it closed for longer. Look, Darrell's actions are desperate. He's doing everything he can to stop the sale. But how is he going to do that? The Oriels are buying the bookstore, and once they do, they'll fix it up, and it'll reopen, and—"

Someone cleared their throat. Looking up, Alice saw a gray-haired couple in matching windbreakers and thick-rimmed glasses. Even though their faces looked nothing alike, the identical clothes and glasses made them look like twins.

"Mr. and Mrs. Oriel," Kris said, smiling. "Are you ready to go see another potential home?"

Mr. Oriel rubbed the back of his neck.

Mrs. Oriel nudged him. "Go ahead. Tell her."

"Tell me what?" Kris looked from Mr. Oriel to Mrs. Oriel and back again.

"It's about the bookstore…" Mr. Oriel said.

"The ghost." Mrs. Oriel shook her head. "It changes everything."

"A ghost?" Kris said. "What ghost?"

"My wife believes—" Mr. Oriel began.

"*We* believe," Mrs. Oriel cut in, correcting her husband. "You're the one that first spotted the one in our old attic. And if it hadn't been for you playing around with that old Ouija board—"

Mr. Oriel raised both hands in a show of surrender. "Guilty as charged."

Mrs. Oriel turned back to Kris. "And don't get us wrong, Miss Cox. We're open-minded. We can tolerate a ghost."

"We can," Mr. Oriel said, nodding, "and we have."

Mrs. Oriel said, "But not *any* ghost. Not *this* ghost."

Kris's mouth was an O of confusion. Finally, she managed to say, "What's wrong with this ghost?"

Mrs. Oriel crossed her arms, frowning, while her husband eyed her nervously.

She said, "I won't have that man, Vince Malone, hanging around our bookstore forever."

"Have you—?" Alice joined the conversation, and feeling that, since they were talking about dead people, she had to drop her voice to a whisper. "Have you seen him?"

Mrs. Oriel shook her head. "I haven't yet. But it's only a matter of time."

"She's very perceptive," Mr. Oriel said. "Always has been."

"You're no slouch, either," Mrs. Oriel said, and gave her husband a playful nudge.

"I don't understand," Kris said. "What does this all mean? Can we do something about the ghost? Uh, get an exorcist?"

Mrs. Oriel snorted. "Exorcists. You've watched too many movies, Miss Cox. No, ghosts simply don't wander off if a priest tells them to. Ghosts stick around until their unfinished business is—is—"

Her husband offered the missing word: "Finished, my dear?"

She smiled at him. "Yes."

"But then…" Kris said in a small voice. "This means…"

Mr. Oriel nodded. "I'm afraid so. We'll have to pull out of the deal. We can't buy Blithedale Books, after all."

CHAPTER 10

*A*lice put her head in her hands. She closed her eyes against the aching throb in her brain.

Too much had happened over the past twenty-four hours: the wedding, her escape, and then coming to Blithedale, which had been an act of desperation.

The bookstore held more than memories. It seemed to contain the last vestiges of her mom and the person Alice ought to have been.

But now that she'd found her hideaway, the bookstore had been closed down, and the only hope of saving it—the Oriels buying and fixing it up—had come crashing down.

She'd watched Kris, stony-faced with shock, follow the Oriels out of the diner on their way to look at a house. Before she could leave, Alice had grabbed the realtor's hand and asked her if there was anything they could do. But Kris had simply shaken her head, staring emptily out into the air.

"Nothing," she'd said. "There's nothing more we can do."

Now Alice was left sitting in the booth wondering if that was true. Alice knew about bookstores—she'd worked in them for years. What could she do?

A hand on her shoulder made her look up. Becca stood over her, her eyebrows bunched together in concern.

"I remember now. I remember who you remind me of."

She put a plate of pancakes in front of Alice with eggs. It was on odd choice of food at this time of day. A small bowl of blueberries sat on the side. Blueberry pancakes with blueberries on the side? A memory stirred. No, not blueberry.

"Cranberry pancakes with blueberries on the side," she whispered, her heart swelling.

Becca smiled. "They were your mom's favorites. My grandma, who ran this diner before I did, used to make them for her. I'll never forget your mom. She was a divine person. So full of love."

Alice stared at the pancakes and felt the tears rising again.

Becca, as if knowing, leaned across the table and pulled several napkins from the dispenser. "Here. Let those tears loose. No point in keeping them locked up."

"You knew her," Alice said, dabbing at her eyes.

"I did," Becca said. "And I knew you. You were such a sweet kid. I used to serve you mango juice. You were crazy about the stuff."

A memory flashed across Alice's mind. "Rebecca!"

Becca laughed. "That's right. Twenty years ago, I had this fascination with my birth name, and it wasn't until I got older and felt more respected that I settled into my natural nickname."

"You used to let me sit at the counter and watch you work."

"Your mom dropped you off sometimes, and I'd keep an eye on you. We all would. All of Blithedale. When your mom —" Becca let out a long, mournful sigh. "Well, it broke everyone's heart. Enough of my reminiscing, you go ahead and eat your pancakes."

Alice did as she was told. The tartness of the cranberries

counterbalanced the sweet maple syrup perfectly. The fried eggs were perfect, too.

"Sunny side up," as her mom liked to say, "because every morning ought to start with sunshine, even if it's raining outside."

That memory led to another, one of Becca, the waitress who had treated a nine-year-old Alice so nicely.

By the time Becca had made the rounds, refilling coffee cups and taking orders, and returned to Alice's booth, Alice had a question.

"Did you once tell me that you were related to a Dickens character?"

Becca laughed. "Nothing wrong with your memory. That's right. Through my maternal line, I can trace my ancestry to Inspector Bucket in *Bleak House*."

"You mean Inspector Bucket was real?"

"Sort of. He was based on a real person. Inspector Field of the Scotland Yard. My grandma always said we had a dash of the inspector's blood in our veins. Now, I have no idea which detective your mom descended from, but I can tell you, she sure had a nose for sleuthing."

"She did?"

"She did. But that's a story for another time. Right now, you'd better go to the inn and get some rest."

"I wish there was something I could do," Alice said with a sigh, settling back into her despair. "But my brain is too tired to think."

"You'll think of something," Becca said. "I suspect you're a lot like your mom, and she always figured out how to solve problems."

Alice nodded. A clock on the wall told her it was already 7 pm. It had been a long, long day.

She dug into her clutch for money, but Becca tsk-tsked. "Your money is no good here. This is my treat."

Too tired to protest at this sign of generosity, Alice simply thanked Becca. Then gathered up the folds of her dress and her clutch and slid out of the booth, the leatherette creaking beneath her. Her heels click-clacked as she hobbled toward the exit and tried hard not to feel bothered by the people staring at her.

As she reached the door, Becca called her name and caught up with her.

"I want you to have this," she said, pressing an envelope into her hands. "Don't open it until you get to the inn. And remember what Charles Dickens wrote, 'The most important thing in life is to stop saying "I wish" and start saying "I will."' Now go get some rest."

CHAPTER 11

*F*ortunately, the Pemberley Inn lay less than a hundred yards from the What the Dickens Diner. As she walked the short distance, Alice's body ached with fatigue, and she wondered what she'd gotten herself into—and how she'd get herself out of it. Should she go back to the city?

She grimaced, hating the idea of crawling back to the city.

Mom never backed down, she thought. *No matter how big the challenges were.*

That thought kept her going as she crossed a bridge over the river that ran through Blithedale and approached the old mansion.

When she'd lived in Blithedale, the place had been a ramshackle house rumored—among kids, at least—to be haunted. Since then, someone had fixed it up. On the surface, however, it only shared a name with Mr. Darcy's country estate from Jane Austen's *Pride & Prejudice*. It was a charming Victorian with a wraparound porch, slate roofing, and a turret with a cockerel weather vane. More New England than England.

By the gate to the front yard stood a bronze statue of a man in a suit. A plaque below said, "Mayor Thomas Reginald Townsend." There was that name again. Townsend. It couldn't be mere coincidence—the Townsend brothers must have old roots in town. Below the plaque was a brass box, its hinged lid hung open. If it had once held an object inside, it was gone now.

At the Pemberley Inn reception, a step inside the front doors, a woman with a patch over one eye was tapping away at a computer. She welcomed Alice with a smile, and didn't even blink her one visible eye at seeing her in a dirty wedding dress.

"You were admiring the statue," the woman said. "Old Mayor Townsend, we call him. He wasn't the first mayor. But he was the first to develop a vision for the town."

"Are Darrell and Todd Townsend related?"

"Only by blood."

The implication wasn't lost on Alice. Old Mayor Townsend's vision apparently had not been passed down.

As the woman found an unoccupied room on the computer, her eyepatch glinted. It was covered in red gemstones.

The woman was focused on the computer screen, but she must have noticed Alice staring, because she said, "They're rhinestones."

"It's beautiful," Alice said, and she meant it.

"Thanks. I like your dress, too. If you need it dry cleaned, I can send it out for you."

Alice gazed down at her outfit. When she'd bolted from the church, she hadn't exactly had a clear plan in mind, let alone considered that she'd need clothes. She didn't even have a tooth brush.

"I need a change of clothes," she said.

"Love Again is down the block. It's a consignment store.

If you go in the morning, Esther Lucas, who runs it, will help you out. Oh, and here."

She reached under the counter and brought up a little pouch. Alice unzipped it and found a toothbrush, toothpaste, shampoo, conditioner, even a tiny hair brush.

"You're a life saver," she said.

Alice handed over her credit card. She did a quick mental calculation. She had plenty of money in her savings, but it wouldn't last forever. She no longer had a job—running out on Rich had meant breaking with her fiancé as well as her boss—and she didn't know when she'd get another. She didn't even know what she'd do tomorrow.

"Can I start by reserving three days?"

"Why don't I note your reservation for a week? If you change your mind, just let me know. No extra cost."

"OK," Alice said, too exhausted to think about what life would look like in a week.

"Alice," the woman said, handing back her credit card. "I'm Ona. I hope you have a nice stay."

Ona led Alice up a set of stairs with an old, polished banister. On the walls hung what at first glance looked like old family portraits, but one of the faces stood out to Alice, and she paused on the steps.

"Is this—?"

Ona nodded. "In his role as Mr. Darcy for the BBC adaptation of *Pride & Prejudice*. He's always been my favorite Darcy."

Alice admired the other tributes to Austen. Each portrait was of a character, often hinting at an actor who'd played the part in a film or TV adaptation. A portrait of Marianne Dashwood hung next to that of her sister, Elinor, and nearby was the dashing Mr. Knightley.

They reached the second floor landing, where a small card table stood with two chairs, and Alice noted that someone had left a game of backgammon half finished. Then realized it must be another Austen artifact. She tried to recall which book would allude to backgammon.

"*Emma?*"

"Very good," Ona said. "Yes, Emma plays backgammon with her father. But how about this one—can you guess what this is?"

A male mannequin stood in a corner. It wore what looked like a cream undershirt, and Alice knew at once what it was.

"That's a flannel waistcoat. Which is actually not what we'd think of as a waistcoat. It's more like long underwear. Colonel Brandon mentions wearing one in *Sense & Sensibility*, and totally turns off Marianne."

Ona laughed. "You know your Jane Austen." She unlocked a door next to the mannequin and said, "As a reward, you'll get the Colonel Brandon Suite."

A four-poster bed dominated the room, but there was also a small escritoire, a chair, and a wardrobe large enough to contain Narnia.

"This is beautiful."

Ona handed her a tourist brochure for the area and a map of town, going on to mention the practical matters: the cost per night, checking out, and the fact that the inn didn't provide breakfast or other meals.

"There's the diner for that. I can't compete with Becca, nor do I want to. Plus, there's a new cafe in town that you might want to try out. Delicious pies."

Alice looked at the tourist brochure. It featured a photo of the old mayor on the front. In the photo, the box was closed.

"What was in that box?"

She pointed. Ona bent over the map.

"Supposedly, the box contained Old Mayor Townsend's journal, in which he noted his ideas for how to develop Blithedale into 'a blissful home for happy souls.' His words, not mine. But about a week ago, someone broke into the box and stole the journal."

"Stole it? Why would anyone steal an old journal? Was it worth a lot?"

"Only to us locals. The old mayor had some great ideas about how to make a town thrive. I heard a rumor that Darrell Townsend might've stolen it simply to erase his great-grandfather's legacy and pave the way—pardon the pun—for his own concrete vision of Blithedale."

"You really think he stole it?"

Ona shrugged. "Maybe. I wouldn't put it past him. And yet..."

"And yet?"

Ona laughed. "Becca called ahead and warned me about you."

Alice was taken aback. "She warned you about me?"

"About you being a natural detective. She thinks you take after your mom, and she apparently solved a bunch of mysteries in town. Anyway, I'll leave you to mull over who stole Old Mayor Townsend's journal."

She bid Alice goodnight and closed the door behind her.

Alice sat on the bed, holding her clutch against her. What was this about her mom solving mysteries? She remembered her mom doing favors for people—was that it? She'd have to ask Becca about it.

She let herself fall backward and stared up at the canopy. Right now, she needed to work out what to do. Old Mayor Townsend's journal meant nothing to her. It was Vince's death that troubled her—if she couldn't do something about the murder, the bookstore might close permanently. It might even fall into the hands of Darrell Townsend, who had no interest in reviving the store Alice's mom had so lovingly created.

Her clutch buzzed, vibrating against her chest. She pulled

her phone out. More missed calls from Rich. Another flurry of texts. They all amounted to the same message: "Where are you? I can come get you, if you'll tell me where you are."

She drafted a reply: "Rich, I'm safe. I'm sorry I hurt you. I need time and space to think. I'll let you know when I'm ready to talk."

That would buy her some time, and hopefully, he wouldn't try too hard to track her down. Though knowing Rich, that was wishful thinking.

She hesitated to hit send, looking at the engagement ring he'd bought her. Then she slipped it off her finger and put it in the drawer of the bedside table.

Raising her phone, she read her message to Rich again. It would have to do. She hit send and shoved the phone back into the handbag.

As she retracted her hand, she felt Becca's envelope.

She raised herself onto one elbow and forced the envelope flap open. Turning it upside down, she shook it, and an object tumbled out.

A key.

Attached to the key by a string was a small, handwritten paper label. It said, "A very little key will open a very heavy door." And then a number, 13.

What could it mean? Alice's brain felt as thick as molasses, but she forced her thoughts forward. A number might be the number on a door.

She slipped off the bed and went out into the hallway.

Her own room was number 14. On the other side of Colonel Brandon, the door was labeled with a brass 13. She tried the key in the lock, but it was all wrong.

"Come on, Alice," she chided herself. "Why would Becca give you a key to one of the rooms at the inn?"

"Wait a minute…" She slapped her forehead. "Of course."

Maybe the key fit a lock in another building.

She rushed back into her room and straight to the escritoire, where she'd left the brochures Ona had given her. She unfolded the map of the town. It was an illustrated map, showing cartoonish versions of the local landmarks. Luckily, the illustrator had numbered the buildings on Main Street.

She let out a little "ha," pleased her theory had been correct.

Number 13 on Main Street was clearly marked.

Blithedale Books.

CHAPTER 12

*a*lice woke in a milky cloud. Her room seemed to have turned a hazy, gauzy white, and what was even stranger was that the mists tickled her nose.

She batted at the mists and swept aside the layers of tulle skirt. She'd slept fully dressed. Apparently, during the night her dress had migrated over her head.

She sat up. Her legs and shoulders and lower back ached. If she'd run a half-marathon—well, at least a 10k run—she couldn't have been more sore. But at least her head no longer pounded.

She slipped off the bed, the skirt flopping to the floor. She went to the escritoire and picked up the key with the paper label, "A very little key will open a very heavy door."

Why had Becca given her a key to Blithedale Books? And what had her parting words meant? "The most important thing in life is to stop saying 'I wish' and start saying 'I will.'"

Alice had an idea. She put the phrase about a very little key into her phone and searched the web. The top search result told her what she needed to know. It was a quote from a story by Charles Dickens. Dickens was Becca's favorite author, so it only made sense that she'd wrap a riddle in his words.

But the riddle wasn't too difficult to understand.

She went to the window and pulled the curtains aside. Bright sunlight poured in and she put a hand up to shield her eyes.

From this side of the Pemberley Inn, she got a good view of Blithedale's Main Street. Forested hills rose toward distant peaks, bluish in the morning light. The seemingly endless woods reached right down to town. A river emerged from the trees, its sparkling waters meandering past the inn. Cars drifted over the bridge. Pedestrians walked along sidewalks that were far cleaner than what she was used to in the city— and with fewer cracks, too. No cockroaches or rats, either.

She pulled open the window and the air rushed in. She half-expected it to be the familiar stench of car exhaust mixed with trash stewing in the sun. But instead it was cool, fresh air. She breathed it in, filling her lungs for what felt like the first time in years.

She leaned over the window ledge, stretching out to get a better view.

Even though she and her mom had lived in Blithedale for several years, her memories were only fragments. She remembered a general store where they sold candy. That had been across from the old Victorian. But it was gone now. There had been an old movie theater—that was still down the street, the old-fashioned marquee advertising *Casablanca*. And hadn't there been an empty lot next to the bookstore? She thought so. But at some point during the past twenty years, another store had gone up. So much had changed— and yet, when she breathed in the fresh air, it was as if she could taste a certain kind of happiness that she remembered from her childhood.

Down below, a man in a suit and tie had stopped to say

hello to a woman walking her dog. A couple walked arm in arm, and they smiled at a kid zipping along the sidewalk on her scooter. The kid called out a "hello, Mr. and Mrs. Jones" over her shoulder.

No one was rushing.

No one was shouldering others aside in a hurry to get to the subway on time.

She was beginning to see why her mom had come here in the first place. The city would've been especially tough for a single mom without any relatives nearby. Had she spotted a bookstore for sale in the classifieds and come for a visit? She must've fallen in love at once.

Across the bridge, a woman held the door open for a man entering the What the Dickens Diner. In the other direction from the inn, there was a place called Dorian's Art Shoppe, and next to that, Love Again. That was the consignment store Ona had mentioned yesterday.

And next to that was Blithedale Books. Number 13.

The sight of it squeezed her heart. It looked closed-up and forlorn. Even at this distance, she could see the closure notice on the door.

She sighed and withdrew from the window.

If Chief Jimbo wouldn't find the killer, then someone else would have to. She remembered what Becca had said about her mom solving mysteries.

What if...?

Don't be silly, a stern voice in her mind told her. *You're using this as an excuse to avoid the real issue: Rich.*

She grabbed her phone and, ignoring both the voice in her mind and the new text messages from Rich, she opened her browser. A quick search confirmed what Kris had told her: Chief Jimbo's closure notice would only last 48 hours. Then the local authorities would need to decide whether the bookstore could reopen. Most likely Darrell Townsend's influence would sway the decision in his favor. She'd seen how he pushed the chief of police around, and apparently the mayor stood to gain from Darrell's plans.

If Alice could find concrete evidence that Vince was murdered, not the victim of a dangerous building, she might influence the outcome. Especially if it turned out to be Darrell who'd pushed Vince. Then the bookstore could reopen. Maybe the Oriels could even be convinced to buy again.

She checked the time. Wow, it was already 9:30 am. She must have slept more than 12 hours. It was Tuesday. By Thursday, Chief Jimbo's 48-hour closure would lapse—or be extended.

She didn't have much time.

Before I can sneak into the bookstore, I'll get cleaned up and change into something more comfortable and—

She shook her head. What was she thinking? She couldn't change into anything. She didn't have any clothes.

Presumably the consignment store would be opening soon, if it wasn't already open.

After washing her face and scrubbing her arm pits with a washcloth, she hurried past the Colonel Brandon mannequin in his flannel undergarment.

Her phone buzzed again, and she stopped on the stairs. She dug out her phone and stared at the screen.

Rich had texted her again. The preview sent a chill down her spine. She opened the message to read the whole thing.

"Everything's going to be OK. I know in my heart that you belong here. You know it, too. I'll find you, my love, and I'll bring you back. I promise."

CHAPTER 13

*I*n Love Again's window display, mannequins wore bright, flowery summer dresses and shorts with tie-dye tank tops. The sign hanging behind the glass of the front door said, "Come in, we're open!"

A bell jingled cheerfully as she stepped inside. From beyond the racks of clothes came a young woman. As she moved toward Alice, she seemed to skim across the floor like a smooth stone on water, her long black hair swaying gracefully behind her. This must be Esther Lucas, the owner Ona had mentioned.

"That's a beautiful dress," Esther said. "Is that a real Vera Wang?"

"No, it's a knockoff. I could never afford a Vera Wang."

Esther laughed, and it sounded like summer raindrops on water. "Who could? But my customers would still kill for a dress like this."

"Personally, I need something a little more practical."

"Like what?"

"Like anything and everything."

"You've come to the right place."

Esther put a hand on a hip and cocked her head, studying Alice. "Let me pick out a few things for you."

While Esther searched the racks, Alice went to check out the footwear section.

A woman in a beige jumpsuit was trying on a pair of white sneakers. Her pre-adolescent daughter sat on a chair reading a graphic novel about a zombie apocalypse. When Alice approached, the girl looked up. She leaned toward her mom and whispered, but it was about as quiet as a stage whisper. Alice heard the words "runaway bride."

"Shush, sweetie. We don't talk about that kind of thing."

The woman gave Alice an apologetic look while the girl scowled. "But daddy was talking about it. He said it was in the news."

That made Alice freeze.

Oh God, no.

She hurried away from the shoes and nearly collided with Esther.

"This way," Esther said, leading her to a changing room.

Esther had her changing into a dozen different outfits, commenting on which ones fit her nicely and which ones were "no go," all the while keeping Alice from looking into the news story the girl had mentioned.

Finally, she'd picked out a whole stack of dresses, pants, shirts, and shorts. It felt great to wear new clothes. She had a pair of jeans, a white tank top, and an open blouse over it. The dirty wedding dress lay in a heap. To her surprise, Esther carried panties and bras, which she also bought several of.

"Yeah, it's a consignment store, but we're also Blithedale's only place for women to buy clothes. So I stock the essentials. Let me bag these items for you. I'll be right back."

As soon as Esther left, Alice dug into her clutch and found her phone and unlocked it. The browser took a moment to load *The Blithedale Record* website. But as soon as the main image appeared, she knew what the girl had been referring to.

The headline read, "Runaway bride witnesses tragic accident." The photo, which Todd Townsend must have snapped without her realizing, showed her from the back as she walked through the diner, heading for the exit, her voluminous skirts darkened with dirt and dust.

What if Rich saw the article? How long would it take him drive to Blithedale and convince her to come back home? If he had his way, she'd be back at that altar tomorrow.

She shuddered.

Esther returned with two well-packed bags.

"What do you want to do about the wedding dress?" she asked. "Do you want a bag for it?"

Alice stared at the wedding dress. She reached out and touched it, running a hand along the fabric. She ought to feel something about it, but she hadn't even chosen it. Not really. When she'd gone wedding dress shopping, it hadn't been with her mom, of course, and since her aunt wasn't an obvious alternative, Rich had said it would be fun to do it together. She'd agreed.

The wedding cake, the music, the floral arrangements, the party favors, the color of table cloths and napkins, the silverware, the catering—they'd looked at everything together. Rich said it was romantic. She'd agreed.

She'd said yes to everything.

And then they were standing at the altar and the minister said, "Do you, Alice Hartford, take Richard Crawley, to be your wedded husband to live together in marriage?" And she realized that for every *yes* she'd given Rich, she actually meant *no*.

Deep down, she'd known she was trapped, yet it took a walk up the aisle of a church for her to finally admit it to herself. She could no longer pretend. She could no longer stay. Not for a single second. Because she knew that if she did, Rich, with his powers of persuasion, would bend her to his will, making her go through with it.

I'll find you, my love, and I'll bring you back.

"I'm not going back," she muttered.

"Not going back where?" Esther asked.

"Never mind," Alice said. She was still holding the hem of the dress, and now she let go. "You can keep it."

"Keep it? Are you serious?"

"I don't ever want to see this dress again."

CHAPTER 14

*A*fter dropping off her bags of clothes at the Pemberley Inn, Alice waited outside of Blithedale Books for an opportunity to sneak in.

Easier said than done. It was broad daylight and, near the front door, a cluster of flowers in tribute to Vince drew every passerby's attention. A wreath made of wildflowers. A votive candle. A hammer with a black ribbon tied around it.

Plus, it seemed every citizen of Blithedale that wasn't ogling the tribute to Vince was staring at Alice. A couple passed and the woman turned around to gaze at her and whisper to her partner.

Even if Alice couldn't hear the words, she knew what they were.

Runaway bride.

Well, once she proved that Vince Malone had been murdered, maybe they'd change their tune.

Amateur detective.

She smiled to herself as she remembered sitting in her hideaway behind the red door, her legs curled up under her and Nancy Drew's *The Clue in the Crumbling Wall* lay open on her lap. She'd devoured Nancy Drew, not to mention the Hardy Boys and Judy Bolton books and dozens of other detective novels. These days, when she picked up a novel, it was more often than not a mystery. Ellery Adams. Elizabeth George. Elly Griffiths.

Maybe there was some truth to what Becca said. Maybe she *had* inherited a talent for detection from her mom. And if she was honest with herself, had she ever truly given up on her childhood dream of solving a real-life mystery?

Here's your chance.

There was a lull in the traffic, and no pedestrians close enough to be paying attention to her.

She moved to the bookstore's front door. As she worked the key into the lock, she couldn't ignore the closure notice. The simple printout had been tacked to the door and said,

"CEASE AND DESIST—all persons are hereby ordered to CEASE and DESIST any and all use and occupancy and to not do any further work on this land or structure."

It was stamped with the Town of Blithedale's seal (a farm-house with a river snaking around it) and signed by Chief Jimbo. It was marked with today's date—Chief Jimbo must have posted it early.

That was good news. She still had almost two full days until the authorities would decide what to do with the book-store. Two days to prove Vince was murdered.

She turned the key and there was an audible click so loud that it made Alice turn and glance up and down the street. Everyone for miles must have heard it.

But, for once, no one was looking her way.

She pulled open the door and slipped inside.

The bookstore was dark. With her back to the door, she got her bearings, getting used to the gloom. Dust and the distinctive smell of musty paper hung heavy in the air. She listened and heard a distant rustling. No doubt mice in the walls. Otherwise it was quiet.

When the contours of the bookshelves came into focus, she moved across the linoleum and down the first aisle. Before she could admit to herself where she was going, she stood by the red door. She ran her fingers over the flaking paint. Something tugged at her heard, and she swallowed, her throat feeling tight. What she wouldn't give to sit inside her hideaway and block out the world and read her books…

But she couldn't hide now. She had a murder mystery to solve.

She turned away from the red door.

Moving through the maze of bookshelves, she made her way to the scaffolding. As she approached it, she slowed down. She dug out her phone and turned on the flashlight and sucked in a breath, expecting to see Vince's body still on the floor.

But of course the body had been removed. She didn't believe in ghosts. The idea didn't spook her in the least.

Besides, the scene of the crime bore no signs of violence. There wasn't even the hint of a blood stain on the floor. The only sign that something was amiss was that the linoleum at the foot of the scaffolding had been scrubbed clean, revealing that it was originally beige instead of brown.

Whoever had cleaned up—she doubted it was Bunce— they had been thorough. It probably meant there wouldn't be any telltale clues.

She gazed up at the top of the scaffolding.

Don't make me go up there.

But of course she had to. There was a metal ladder fastened to the side of the scaffolding, making it easy enough to climb. She grabbed one of the metal rungs and put her foot on the bottom one and took a deep breath.

With every step she took, the whole structure shook.

In fiction, detectives climbed towers, leaped from one roof to another, and jumped off balconies, only to land safely on cafe awnings. As a reader, she'd shared their confidence. Now she felt none. Maybe if she'd been more committed to reading nonfiction, she'd have a better sense of the dangers of scaffolding. What were the accident rates for these rickety things, anyway?

Halfway up, she had to stop and breathe deeply to stave off a panic attack. What if she'd been wrong? What if unsafe scaffolding had killed Vince, and she was about to join him? Another ghost haunting Blithedale Books…

She was seriously considering climbing back down, when she heard the front door open. She froze. Then realized how exposed she was, and forgetting all about unsafe scaffolding, she scurried up the ladder and threw herself over the top. She landed on the platform with a clatter. Then lay still, her breath gushing in her ears, as loud as Niagara Falls.

"Did you hear something?" a voice said. It was Bunce.

"A ghost?" The other man laughed. "Don't tell me you've become superstitious, too. Come on, let's take a look around before anyone finds out we're here."

Alice recognized the voice, and peering over the edge of the scaffolding she confirmed it. Even in the gloom, she recognized Bunce's hunched over figure and, next to him, the bulky man in a business suit.

Darrell Townsend.

CHAPTER 15

*W*hat was Darrell Townsend doing in Blithedale Books—and why had Bunce let him into the store? "I'd rather the ceiling collapsed on me than sell to that viper," Bunce had said, and yet here he was, secretly letting Darrell into the store.

Alice raised her head over the edge of the scaffolding platform to peer down at them. Bunce had retreated to stand behind the counter, as if he felt safer back there, and he'd crossed his arms on his chest.

"Take a look around," Bunce said. "Ask me what you want. But make it quick. If Chief Jimbo catches us in here…"

"Don't worry about Chief Jimbo. I'll take care of him."

Darrell looked around the space, eventually turning his gaze upward, and for an instant, he seemed to look straight at her. Alice ducked. She hoped the gloom hid her well enough.

Footsteps scuffed across the linoleum.

"Old air conditioning units. The floor will have to go." There was a loud metallic banging. "Pipes look rusty."

"The pipes are fine," Bunce snapped.

"I'll take your word for it," Darrell said. "How about the walls?"

"You're buying the store as is. That's the deal. Or there's no deal."

"I wouldn't have it any other way, Bunce."

"And no tearing down the store and building a parking lot."

Darrell laughed. "If I didn't know you better, Bunce, I'd think you were sentimentally attached to the bookstore."

Bunce mumbled something Alice couldn't hear.

"Of course, it's your town, too," Darrell said. "Although not for long, eh? Once you retire to Florida, you can stop worrying about what happens in Blithedale. Anyway, you can rest assured that I'll honor your request. So long as I don't find any structural damage that would require me to demolish the place…"

"I've told you, there's no structural damage. That's a nonsense rumor your brother's spread, and you know it."

"As long as we're in agreement…"

Bunce sighed. "Yes, yes, we're in agreement. And we'll put it in writing."

"You don't trust me, do you, Bunce?"

"I'll sell to you, Mr. Townsend. But I won't ever trust you."

"Fair enough. Still, as gentlemen, we can shake on it."

Alice peeked over the edge again and saw, to her horror, that Darrell had reached a hand across the counter. Bunce took it and they shook.

"Congratulations, Bunce. Your dream of retiring to Florida is about to become reality."

Darrell turned his back on Bunce and, standing with his hands on his hips, surveyed the store. A smile spread across his face.

CHAPTER 16

$\mathcal{T}$he front door closed and there was a loud snick-snick as Bunce locked it from the outside. Alice lay still for a moment. Her heart beat heavily in her chest. Kris must have told Bunce that the Oriels weren't buying the bookstore after all, and he'd gone straight to Darrell.

So much for his promise never to sell to the developer.

But if no one else wanted to buy the bookstore, could she blame him? At least Bunce had extracted a promise that Darrell wouldn't tear down the bookstore. That was something. And if they put it in writing, maybe there would be a way to ensure Darrell didn't break that promise. Though Bunce hadn't insisted Darrell continue to run a bookstore. Darrell would gut the place—she had no doubt about that. Everything would go: Bookshelves. Flooring. And, worst of all, her beloved hideaway with the red door.

She got on her knees and then, cautiously grabbing the railing, stood. She felt wobbly—or the entire scaffolding did —and she wondered how Vince had felt working up here.

She stretched out a hand and touched the ceiling. The scaffolding was also close enough to the back wall that she could easily touch that too. A vein of spackle showed where Vince had filled in a crack—the leak he'd been fixing. It looked as if he'd almost finished.

Vince's toolbox still stood at this end of the platform. A hammer and chisel lay next to it. The platform was covered in dust, but the worst of it—with chunks of crumbly mortar —lay in a heap at the other end. She supposed Vince must've swept the cement aside while he was working.

She examined it closer, sifting through it with her hands, and hoping to discover something hidden inside the cement dust. Nothing. She straightened up and shook her head. What had she expected, a polaroid photo showing the killer in action? This detective work wouldn't be so easy.

With no real insights from the scaffolding, she decided to climb down. She descended slowly, carefully, her chest constricting whenever the metal structure shook and wobbled.

She was only a few rungs down when she happened to raise her gaze from her feet and saw something glinting, dangling from a diagonal brace. She cocked her head. It looked like a chain...

She reached her hand through the gap in the ladder. It was too far. She put one foot on a scaffolding beam and stepped off the ladder, still holding on with both hands. This brought her closer. But now she had to let go of the ladder with her left hand, so she could try to grab the object dangling from the brace.

She took a deep breath.

And let go.

She gripped the ladder hard with her right hand as she swayed on the beam, feeling like a tightrope walker. Her heart leapt into her throat. She tried to breathe slowly, but it felt as if her throat was blocking off the air.

Come on. You can do this.

She reached out, stretching her arm toward the chain.

Her fingertips brushed it and it swung away from her.

Just a little closer…

She leaned farther out. There was nothing below her but metal braces and the hard linoleum floor.

Don't look down.

She focused her attention on the chain. Her right hand, growing moist with sweat, slipped, and she gasped. Her left foot almost slipped. She pulled back and grabbed the ladder with both hands, her heart hammering against her chest, her throat burning.

If I fall…

She forced herself to look straight ahead. Looking down would only spook her more. She inhaled. She wiped off her right hand on her pants.

It's now or never…

She released her left hand from the ladder and stepped further out on the beam. Gripping the ladder firmly, she leaned out as far as she could. Her arm muscles strained. Her right hand was already getting slippery again.

Her left fingertips brushed the chain. Her right hand slid along the metal ladder rung. A couple more seconds and she'd lose her grip.

But she was so close…

Her right hand slid again, two fingers coming loose. She held on with her ring finger and pinkie, nothing else, as she lunged at the chain. Her right hand snagged it, and she pulled back just as her ring and pinkie fingers slipped off the rung. For an instant, she stood on the metal scaffolding beam without holding onto anything.

Then she began to flail, her hands turning in wild circles to keep her balance. Gravity tugged at her shoulders, urging her backward. Her heels slipped off the metal beam. She was falling backward.

Whipping out her right hand, she slammed the palm of her hand onto hard metal and she closed her fist—with a cry of relief, she felt cold metal against her fingers.

And then she fell.

Her feet flew off the metal beam, and the world spun.

But her right-handed grip on the ladder stopped her fall.

Instead, she swung back against the scaffolding, slamming into the ladder. A metal bar dug into her ribs. She cried out.

She panted. Blinked away tears of pain. Then, looking down at the floor below, she laughed, so relieved to be dangling off the ladder.

Feet back on the ladder, she pulled herself close, hugging the metal ladder, still laughing with relief.

She raised her left fist, in which she clutched the chain.

Hello, shiny little thing, she thought, *you'd better be worth the fall...*

CHAPTER 17

"$\mathcal{W}$hy, that's pretty," Becca said as she moved up the diner counter and refilled Alice's coffee cup. "Where did you get it?"

"Someone must have dropped it."

In fact, that was the conclusion she'd come to over lunch at the diner. But she thought it better not to mention where she'd found it.

Becca leaned forward and dropped her voice to a whisper. "You found it in the bookstore, didn't you?"

Alice hesitated. Who could she trust—and who couldn't she? Becca was the one who'd nudged her into investigating. She'd given her the key to the bookstore. She could be an important ally in tracking down the killer.

"You're right," Alice said. "I found it where Vince died. Do you recognize it?"

Becca took the necklace and held it up to the light.

"Simple gold chain. The rings are small, which might be more typical of a woman's necklace, but honestly, this could've been worn by a man, too." She raised an eyebrow at Alice. "You think the killer dropped this?"

"It's possible."

She told Becca about finding it dangling from a beam, and Becca nodded. "Maybe Vince struggled with his attacker and tore this off."

"Exactly. The chain falls off, but when the killer searches the floor, they can't find it—because it's caught on the scaffolding."

"It makes sense," Becca said. Then, with a sigh, she handed Alice the necklace again. "But it's speculation. It doesn't confirm that there was a killer, let alone who the killer was. Though I suppose the killer might worry they'd left behind some evidence."

"And they'd come back," Alice said, nodding.

At first, Becca seemed to have doubted that Alice saw someone run from the bookstore when Vince died. But her doubts had clearly vanished, and it convinced Alice to take her further into her confidence. She shared what she'd witnessed in the bookstore—the deal between Bunce and Darrell.

Becca gave a low whistle. "Things are moving fast. The Oriels have barely walked away from the deal and Darrell's already swooped in. But honestly, I don't know why I should be surprised. That man usually gets what he wants."

"And if he doesn't?"

"Oh, he makes sure that he does."

Alice sipped her coffee, considering what she'd learned so far. Her best lead was the necklace.

"Where would someone buy a necklace like this?"

Becca shrugged. "Love Again carries jewelry. You might want to check with the owner, Esther."

Becca looked at the chain again. "Like a gold string. In *Barnaby Rudge*, Dickens wrote, 'There are strings in the human heart that had better not be vibrated.'" She gave Alice a meaningful look. "You'd better be careful."

CHAPTER 18

$\mathcal{E}$sther Lucas showed Alice a revolving rack with simple chains in silver and gold. The gold ones looked identical to what she'd found.

"I've got pendants that go with them," Esther explained, pointing out another rack, which held hearts, stars, and other shapes you could attach to the necklace.

"Someone dropped this one," Alice explained. "How would I find the owner?"

"Apart from asking everyone in town?" Esther shrugged. "Honestly, if someone doesn't ask around to see if their necklace has been found, I don't see how you can tell. It's a simple necklace. Nothing unique about it."

"Do you remember selling a necklace like that recently?"

"Sure. I sell a lot of them. They're a good gift item. I'd say half of Blithedale has bought one at some point and almost always with one or more pendants. Even I wear one…"

She unbuttoned the top of her blouse, revealing a necklace. It was identical to the one Alice had found.

"See how I've strung together several pendants?" Three stars hung from the gold chain. "Customers love to tailor the gift. Though I will say that women tend to be more creative than men. Some men default to hearts, thinking it's the only romantic option."

A thought occurred to Alice. What if the killer had worn a necklace with pendants? When the chain came undone, they would have fallen off and tumbled to the floor. Maybe the killer had managed to collect them before running out. Or maybe not. In which case, they lay hidden somewhere in the shadows.

She might have to sneak into Blithedale Books again to take another look around.

She thanked Esther and headed toward the exit, only to stop herself at the door. An idea niggled at the back of her mind.

"Esther, you said some men defaulted to hearts because it was romantic. So they were gifts?"

"Almost always. I got customers like Vince—" She put a hand to her chest and cast her eyes down in a gesture of respect, then carried right on talking: "—who bought several, each time choosing a single heart. But then I was surprised when an older guy came in and bought a chain, and he said it was for himself. He got a pendant with a dollar sign."

Alice's heart beat faster. Pieces of the puzzle were coming together, and they all had dollar signs on them.

"It wasn't Darrell Townsend, was it?"

"Wow, how did you know that?"

"Lucky guess."

CHAPTER 19

*I*f you want to know who committed a crime, take a look at who benefits the most.

That was what Alice was thinking after leaving Esther's store. Vince's death had resulted in the bookstore shutting down, the Oriels pulling out of the deal, and Bunce caving in to Darrell's offer to buy.

So who was benefitting the most from Vince's death?

The answer was obvious: Darrell.

Once her suspicion settled on him, she realized she'd felt it all along. Here was a guy who would go to great lengths to get what he wanted, even coercing the local police chief to shut down the bookstore.

The question was whether he still wore the necklace he'd bought from Esther. Or was it the one balled up in Alice's pocket?

At the What the Dickens Diner, she asked Becca about Darrell and learned where to find the offices of his company, Townsend Development. She also learned that Darrell usually left work around 6 pm.

"He's divorced and lives alone in a big house in the

woods," Becca explained. She frowned. "Hold on, Alice. You aren't planning to do a stakeout, are you?"

Alice winced and looked around, worried someone had overheard them. In her excitement, Becca had forgotten to keep her voice down, emphasizing the word *stakeout.*

"I need to find out if he's wearing a necklace," Alice whispered.

"And if he isn't?"

"Then I'll…"

Alice frowned. She wasn't sure what she'd do. If Esther had sold dozens of identical necklaces, it would be impossible to prove that the one she'd found was Darrell's.

"Well, at least I'll be one step closer."

"Closer to what? Finding evidence against Darrell Townsend?" Becca pursed her lips. "Alice, you'd better know what you're doing, because the Darrell Townsends of this world don't take kindly to false accusations."

"I thought you were encouraging me to investigate."

"I am. I just worry…" She sighed. "I can hardly stop you. Your mom got into a whole heap of trouble, and I wouldn't have wished her to hold back."

Alice bit her lip. "Becca, you mentioned my mom solved some mysteries…"

"Your mom was a natural," Becca said. "And so are you. I'm sure of it. But that doesn't mean it's not dangerous work. Speaking of work, I'd better bring this check to table four. And Lenny over there will want more coffee."

Becca grabbed the pot of coffee. "Alice? Promise me you'll be careful."

"I promise, I will be."

Alice tried to smile and look confident, though she felt about as self-assured as a baby doe taking its first wobbly steps. She headed toward the exit, making sure to stride with confidence, and ignoring the desire to glance back over her shoulder.

When she got to the front door, she pulled hard. Confident. The door rattled but didn't budge. She tried again. Extra confident. Extra hard.

Nothing.

A small sign in the window told her to "PUSH."

"Crap," she muttered to herself.

She glanced back at Becca, who was eyeing her with undisguised sympathy. And a lot of worry.

CHAPTER 20

Townsend Development occupied a building on Main Street that didn't belong in Blithedale. A square of glass and steel, it looked as if someone had lopped off the top of a city skyscraper and dumped it between the Blithedale municipal building and the public library.

Passing the parking lot out front, she pretended to be sauntering by as she studied the cars. It didn't take her long to guess which one belonged to Darrell. It was a large, black SUV with vanity license plates that said, "DRL 4EVR."

Past the public library, she stopped. She needed to watch the front of the building to spot Darrell coming out. Across from Townsend Development lay a small cafe called Bonsai & Pie.

Alice crossed the street.

Inside, the cafe was tiny. The only seating was a row of four stools under a counter by the window. Behind that, the glass display nearly spanned the width of the room with lots of pies on display. A tabletop fountain sat on the counter, with water cascading down three tiers of granite rock.

The thing that stood out the most, however, was that

every other surface—from the counter to shelves along the walls—held pots or trays with distinctive, miniature trees. Bonsais.

There were tiny pine trees, one that looked like a maple, and another with beautiful white flowers.

Turning her attention to the glass counter, Alice bent down to take a look at the pies. Key lime pie. Apple. Cherry. Coconut cream. Georgia peach. Strawberry and rhubarb. Sweet potato. Chocolate pecan. There was even a tiramisu.

"See anything you like?"

At the sound of the woman's voice, Alice straightened up. The woman had a shaved head, dreamcatcher earrings, and a loose tie-dyed dress.

"Did you make all these?"

"Yes, and the bonsais, too."

The woman made a sweeping gesture, and Alice looked around at the bonsai trees again. A couple stood on the window counter, one on the glass case, and the rest on wall shelving. All told, there must be more than a dozen.

"So many," Alice said. "And they all look different."

"That's a juniper. And that one's a Japanese maple." The woman gave Alice a sad smile. "But look at me, gabbing away. I love bonsais and could talk about them for hours. I'm Andrea, by the way, and you must be Alice."

"Nobody's a stranger in a small town, huh?"

Andrea nodded. "Plus, you made a dramatic entrance in a wedding dress."

Alice couldn't deny that. She ordered a cup of coffee and settled onto a stool by the window. She had a clear view of Darrell's workplace as well as his car.

She sipped her coffee. A man left the building and got into a Lexus and backed out of the lot. She watched the car turn onto Main Street and drift away. If that had been Darrell, she wouldn't have been able to check if he was wearing a necklace or not. And because she didn't have a car, she couldn't follow. She took a sip of coffee and considered how she could get closer.

The door to the cafe opened and a woman entered.

"Here you go, Lorraine," Andrea said, handing the woman a pie box.

"Oh, the book club ladies will be so pleased. Your key lime is everyone's favorite."

The woman hurried out and Alice watched her cross the street and climb the steps to the public library. She guessed Lorraine was a librarian bringing her friends a treat for afternoon coffee. And that gave her an idea.

"Andrea, what's your most popular pie?"

"Apple crumble. It's a crowd pleaser."

Alice drained her coffee and slid off the stool.

"One apple crumble to go."

CHAPTER 21

*T*he reception area of Townsend Development felt like any corporate waiting room Alice had ever set foot in: icy, dry air courtesy of air conditioning, bluish gray carpeting, and straight-backed chairs and a couple of small couches around a coffee table with neatly arranged magazines. A single potted palm, a half-hearted nod to nature, stood in a corner.

As Alice entered, the receptionist looked up and smiled.

"Do you have an appointment, miss?"

"Much better," Alice said. "I have pie."

She put the pie box on the receptionist's desk.

The woman stared at the box and frowned.

"I wasn't aware that we'd ordered pie."

"You didn't." Alice put on her most winning smile. "But you all work hard here at Townsend Development, and I thought you could use a treat. It's apple crumble. Everyone's favorite."

The woman studied the box. Then, picking up a pen, she pushed the pie box away from her.

"I can't eat gluten."

"Oh." Alice's smile faltered. "But maybe someone else at the office does? Like Darrell?"

The woman turned to her computer and typed on the keyboard, her fake nails clacking noisily. "I'm so sorry, but Mr. Townsend is booked solid for the rest of the afternoon. So…"

"So?"

"So, goodbye, and have a nice day."

Alice's heart sank. Her plan had seemed perfect—exactly what a detective would do in a novel. Why did it always work out for the heroines in books?

She turned to go, but was stopped by the woman clearing her throat. The receptionist pointed at the pie box as if it contained plutonium.

"Don't forget that thing."

Alice picked up the box and, swinging around, collided with a man.

"Careful!" he said.

Alice lost her grip on the box, but the man reached in and grabbed it in time.

"Phew," Alice said. "Thanks."

She looked up and recognized him. It was Darrell's tall, lanky brother, Todd, owner of *The Blithedale Record*.

Todd smiled. "The runaway bride again. And what's this?" He looked over her shoulder at the receptionist. "Janice, did you order pie?"

"Did I order a cake full of gluten? No, I did not," Janice answered.

"I brought it," Alice said. "It's a gift."

Todd opened the box. "Apple crumble." He raised an eyebrow at Alice. "This isn't a gift. This is a bribe." Then he grinned. "Darrell and I never say no to apple crumble. Come on."

With one hand holding the pie box, he put the other

around her shoulders, as if they were old friends, and led her past the reception—and Janice's deep frown—to double doors at the back.

Todd let go of Alice and pushed open one of the doors.

"Brother," he called out. "Look who I caught trying to bribe her way into your office."

CHAPTER 22

*D*arrell Townsend sat behind a massive see-through desk. It must've been made of acrylic. His office chair was white. The walls at either end of the room were white, too, including where Alice and Todd had entered through the double doors. The other two walls were glass, one providing a view on the street, the other, behind Darrell, looking out at dense forest.

Darrell placed his elbows on the desk and steepled his fingers.

"What an unexpected pleasure. What's this about a bribe?"

Todd, grinning, tossed the pie box onto the desk, and then threw himself onto one of the chairs facing the desk. He was so long-legged, he looked like a giraffe on a dollhouse chair.

Darrell lifted the lid on the pie box and raised an eyebrow.

"Apple crumble. Highly suspicious." He gestured at Alice. "Please, take a seat."

Alice was staring at Darrell's neck. His button-down shirt

was buttoned up. There was no way of telling whether he wore a necklace or not.

She sat down.

Darrell pressed a button on his desk phone. "Janice, bring us coffee. Three. All black. And three plates with spoons and a cake knife, please."

He studied Alice. "Do you know how I know that you prefer black coffee?"

Alice shook her head.

"Because it's my business to know what goes on in Blithedale."

Janice entered the office with a tray. She put the plates down, one near each of them, and then the cups of black coffee. She handed Darrell the cake knife. As she turned, she gave Alice a parting glance, barely disguising her sneer.

Once Janice had closed the door behind her, Darrell opened the box and cut the pie. He dished out a slice for Alice, one for Todd, and one for himself. Alice noted that Darrell had cut a slightly larger piece for himself.

"As I was saying," he said, settling back into his chair, "I know what goes on in this town, and I know who comes and who goes. I even know—" He forked up a mouthful of pie and chewed it, closing his eyes, obviously savoring the taste. "—which pie is the best in town."

Alice hadn't touched her coffee or her pie. Todd was eating his apple crumble with gusto, washing down big mouthfuls with coffee. But between bites, he glanced over at Alice and at his brother, constantly alert to what was going on.

"This is good pie," Darrell said. "In fact, it's the best in Blithedale. But some day, we will have half a dozen cafés with delicious pies. Some day, Blithedale will be known as the pie capitol."

"Though probably not the bonsai capitol," Todd quipped, and snickered.

Darrell smiled. "Probably not. Small stores like Bonsai & Pie represent baby steps. When Blithedale grows up, the town will offer something no other town for miles can offer —the amenities of the city surrounded by nature. Modern condos. Mansions with four-car garages. Big box stores by a sparkling river. Widescreen movie theaters nestled in the woods. Shopping malls where once there were farms."

"Sounds like a big vision for the distant future," Alice said.

Actually, it sounded like a dystopian future, but she didn't say that.

"Not as distant as you might think. Within a decade, this town will be transformed. But it will take work. And it will take change. But you're no stranger to change, are you, Miss Hartford?"

He touched a mouse on his desk and stared at the computer screen, its contents hidden from Alice's view.

"Alice Hartford, 29 years old. Unmarried. Engaged to be married to one Richard Crawley. Also known as 'Rich.' Owner of Crawley Books, one of the city's most well-regarded independent bookstores, where Alice Hartford worked as a bookstore manager, reporting to—oh, a little office romance—Rich Crawley himself. In fact, there was a big wedding planned for a few days ago, and then…" Darrell raised his hands in a mock display of confusion. "…nothing. No social media posts. No gushing about the wedding. But coincidentally, a runaway bride appears many miles away in a small town called Blithedale, selling her wedding dress at a consignment store. And taking an unusual interest in a bookstore, of all places."

He tsk-tsked, shaking his head.

"This love story has taken a shocking turn. The poor

groom apparently doesn't even know where his bride has run off to."

An icy feeling crept down Alice's spine. Darrell's crocodile smile made her insides cold, too.

"What are you saying?"

"I'm saying that Rich Crawley might appreciate a little information on where his bride has gone."

"Leave Rich out of this."

"Out of what, Miss Hartford? I'm only suggesting I'd be doing a good deed. Helping out a broken-hearted man."

"What do you want, Darrell?"

He clicked his mouse and turned away from the screen, facing her again.

"You seem unusually interested in Blithedale Books."

"A man died there," Alice said.

"Yes, you supposedly saw Vince's killer. I've heard your story. It doesn't get any more plausible with each retelling."

"I'm not lying."

"If you're such an honest person, why break into the bookstore and eavesdrop on Bunce and myself?"

Darrell raised an eyebrow, challenging her to answer.

Alice tensed. He had looked straight at her, yet in the gloom of the bookstore, she'd been so sure he hadn't spotted her. She'd been wrong.

She pressed her lips shut, refusing to confirm his accusation, but also seeing no point in denying it.

"Alice," he said with a sigh. "May I call you Alice? Of course I may. Listen, whether you have a need to play amateur sleuth or some unhealthy obsession for a ramshackle bookstore, I don't have time for people who meddle in my affairs. Do you understand?"

"You're telling me to back off. Do you know how incriminating that is?"

Darrell smiled and looked at his brother. "See? I told you she'd be reasonable."

Todd shrugged. "She did just accuse of you of breaking the law."

"There's nothing incriminating about buying a bookstore that no one else wants to buy. Besides, Todd, what is it I keep telling you?"

"The law can bend so far, why bother breaking it?"

Darrell wagged his cake fork at Todd, while smiling at Alice. "Careful with this guy. Once you tell him something, he never forgets." He pointed at her plate with the piece of untouched pie. "Are you going to eat that?"

Alice shook her head.

"You can see yourself out," he said as he leaned across the desk and took the plate, bringing it over to his side. For an instant, she had a clear view down his shirt at his collarbone. A glint of gold caught her eye. A necklace.

She clenched her fists, and leaned forward to get a better look. Yes, the necklace was like the one she had in her pocket. Identical. Except a pendant dangled from it...

She sank back in her chair, letting out a disappointed sigh.

The pendant wasn't a heart. It was a little gold dollar sign.

CHAPTER 23

*B*ack at the Pemberley Inn, Alice threw herself down on her bed.

She stared up at the canopy, thinking over what she'd learned. She couldn't concentrate. Every time she thought of Vince's murder and the clues she'd gathered so far, Rich's face swam into her mind, interrupting, and she thought she heard her phone buzz again.

When she checked the phone, the lock screen notified her of more missed calls and messages, but nobody was calling her now.

She lay back down with a sigh.

Darrell's threat to contact Rich had rattled her. She didn't know what she'd say or do if Rich showed up. But the fact that Darrell had threatened her, didn't that, more than anything else, suggest that he was guilty?

And yet there was the necklace…

It didn't prove or disprove anything that Darrell wore a necklace. Still, it was a blow to her theory that he'd murdered Vince to get his hands on the bookstore.

She closed her eyes. If only she could find concrete evidence that Darrell was guilty…

Thump, thump, thump.

A banging from outside made her open her eyes. She got off her bed and went to the window. Out in the street, cars drifted past, people hurried along the sidewalk on their way home from work, and above the rooftops the afternoon sun was sinking in the sky.

She couldn't see where the banging was coming from, but it continued.

On the staircase landing, she stopped and listened.

Thump, thump, thump.

It might be coming from out back.

At the bottom of the stairs, she expected to see Ona in the reception, but the counter was abandoned, a small chalkboard stood on an easel. The chalk letters said,

Be back soon—or find me out back.

The hallway led straight from the front door to a common room at the back. This might once have been a dining room. Oriental rugs covered lacquered hardwood floors. A French window opened onto the backyard. Once, this must have been dominated by a long dining table, offering a view of the outside—not to mention direct access to a game of croquet.

These days, however, it was a place for inn guests to sit in armchairs and read books or play boardgames at one of several round tables.

Alice examined the bookshelves. There were several sets of the collected works of Jane Austen. She picked out a hardbound edition of *Persuasion* to reread later.

Then she studied the many games stacked on the shelves.

There were Austen-themed puzzles, a board game called *Polite Society*, and another titled *Lizzy Loves Darcy: A Jane Austen Matchmaking Game*.

Thwack, thwack, thwack.

Alice turned toward the hammering. The sound was closer now, and she could tell that it must be a hammer on wood. She opened the French doors and stepped onto a porch.

The sight that met her made her stop in her tracks.

The Pemberley Inn had a long backyard, which would once have been perfect, as she'd guessed, for croquet. But there was no room for games now. Because the entire backyard was filled with tiny houses—like a miniature village.

CHAPTER 24

*E*ach tiny house was obviously big enough for an adult to live in, yet so small it couldn't be more than 300 or 400 square feet. The miniature houses made Alice think of her namesake from Wonderland and the bottle that said "drink me." It was as if a village of pretty houses had all drunk a shrinking potion.

The variety of architectural styles was staggering. Victorian, Edwardian, Neoclassical. There was a miniature log cabin. One with a straw roof. Another looking like modern Scandinavian architecture with large windows and unpainted pine wood.

As Alice followed the sound of the thwack, thwack, thwack, she admired the handiwork, smiling at the painstaking detail the builder had put into making these homes.

In the middle of the village, Alice came to a clearing, and there stood Ona, holding a long plank across two sawhorses as she hammered a chisel into the wood.

She stopped and looked up. She lifted a pair of work

goggles to her forehead, uncovering her naked eye and her glittering eyepatch.

She smiled. "Why so surprised—you don't have a hobby?"

Alice laughed and held up the book. "My hobby is more modest. I read books."

"You enter fantasy worlds," Ona said. "I create fantasy homes."

"You can say that again."

Alice caught sight of a nearby house that was all rounded edges and circles, like a giant barrel on its side. The door was round, and bore a striking resemblance to Bilbo Baggins's home in *The Hobbit*.

"I've read about tiny houses but never actually seen them in person. Can you live in these?"

"Of course you can," Ona said. "Come on, I'll show you."

Ona put down her hammer, took the goggles off entirely, and led Alice into the nearest tiny house.

"This is my showroom," Ona said.

From the outside, the tiny house had looked—well, tiny. But once Alice stepped inside, she was amazed by how spacious it felt. A full kitchen dominated the left side. There was an L-shaped hardwood counter top, modern appliances, including a full-sized fridge and freezer unit. A small table sat in the middle with two chairs tucked under it.

On the other side was the living room space. Admittedly, compared with a normal living room this was tiny, with a love seat and an arm chair jostling for space with a wood-burning stove. But instead of feeling cramped, it felt cozy.

Ona opened a small door. "There's a small patio out here. And let me show you the bedroom."

She opened a door off the kitchen. A queen-sized bed fit snugly into a room with art prints on the walls and ledges holding scented candles and wooden figurines.

"Cute," Alice said, and meant it.

"And this door leads to the bathroom."

"Wow, there's even a washer-dryer. How big is this place?"

Ona laughed. "That's what people always ask at this point. Impressive how many amenities you can pack into 425 square feet, huh?"

Alice walked through the small space again, admiring the way everything fit. "I've seen houses three times this size that feel less convenient. You built this yourself? That's impressive."

Ona tipped her head, acknowledging the compliment.

"So what's the catch?" she asked.

Ona smiled. "Spoken like a true cynic. But you're right, there is a catch. Tiny houses are still a newfangled thing, and not every town zoning board is eager to change the rules to allow such small houses to be built, let alone lived in."

She explained how building codes often mandated that homes be a certain size for safety reasons. "But those regulations were created when all houses were over 500 square feet. With tiny houses, we've all got to change how we view the idea of living space. Or office space, since businesses can use the houses, too. Sometimes it means making more use of the outdoors—and isn't that a wonderful idea when you live surrounded by woods?" She sighed. "That's my pitch, anyway. People love the idea. They love my houses. But every time someone plans to buy a tiny house and put it on a property in Blithedale, the authorities stop them."

"Chief Jimbo?"

"Jimbo doesn't care. It's Mayor MacDonald who isn't a fan, and in the end, he has to change the development code to allow tiny houses to be used as homes or businesses. Let's just say that the town's top realtor isn't thrilled about a movement that encourages fewer square meters and lower costs. Outside of the town center, the code is more flexible.

So my customers are people who live in the woods. But that's not a big customer base. As you can see," she said, as she led Alice back out into the village of tiny houses, "I can build more than I can sell."

"They're amazing," Alice said, impressed. "I wish I could live in one of your tiny houses. And some of these are so magical, I can imagine a store or other business inside too."

Ona looked at Alice, then checked her watch. "You busy? No? Good. I've got something I want to show you."

She led Alice back through the inn. At the reception, she wiped off the chalkboard and wrote "Need help? Call me," putting a number below it.

Outside, Ona gestured for Alice to get into a pickup truck.

When they'd settled into their seat and Ona turned on the engine, she gave Alice a big grin. "Prepare to be amazed."

CHAPTER 25

The Woodlander Bar lay just off one of the main roads cutting through the forest. As soon as Ona pulled her pickup truck into the gravel parking lot, Alice saw the owner must be one of her customers.

In a clearing stood a tiny house. Shade sails strung between the trees sheltered a dozen tables, giving the place a beach bar vibe—if that beach happened to be located in the middle of the woods.

Speakers played a chilled-out bluegrass soundtrack, setting the perfect mood. As Ona slammed the door to the truck, a man emerged from the tiny house, ducking under the low lintel. He was a tall dude with long, blonde hair. He wore surfer shorts and a baggy, flowery shirt.

"Ona!" he called out and advanced on them.

Ona introduced Alice to the bar owner. His name was Thor.

"Like the Norse God of Thunder?" Alice asked.

"In my defense," Thor said with a smile, "my parents are from Denmark, and it's a pretty common name there.

Without the H, though. But hey, you didn't come to hear about my origins. What do you want to drink?"

They ordered Thor's signature cocktail, an old fashioned —whiskey, bitters, and sugar—with an infusion of pine giving it a rustic flavor.

Sitting down, Alice and Ona talked about the bar and the tiny house, and soon Ona was telling Alice about her own decision to move to Blithedale many years ago.

"I won't bore you with the long sob story, but let's just say that I ran from a poor relationship. When I heard about you —a runaway bride—coming to town, I was reminded of my first day in Blithedale."

Ona sipped her drink and studied Alice for a moment.

"It made me want to meet you and make sure I could help you in any way possible."

"You're helping me right now, Ona. I haven't had a drink with a friend like this since forever."

They clinked glasses and drank. A warm feeling spread through Alice's limbs, and the potent cocktail wasn't the only reason. She'd been honest with Ona. It had been a long time since she'd had a good friend she could talk to, and she already liked Ona so much.

As they drank and talked, the shadows lengthened in the woods, and Thor lit hurricane lanterns at the edge of the clearing and candles on the tables. More and more people showed up, including, Alice noted, Mr. and Mrs. Oriel.

She studied them from afar. They were deeply engaged in a conversation and didn't seem to notice the people around them. Soon, Ona drew Alice back into their own conversation.

Alice appreciated that Ona didn't ask personal questions, maybe sensing that runaway brides had no desire to share all their secrets. At least this runaway bride didn't. So they talked about Blithedale and tiny houses and the blessings of a good cocktail bar.

A car pulled up to the gravel parking lot near the bar and a man got out. He caught Alice's attention at once, because of the white suit he wore. He was past middle age, with unruly white hair under a straw hat, and as he sauntered her way, leaning on a walking stick, she had the crazy notion that Mark Twain had stepped through a time portal. Even the mustache was a perfect match.

As he was passing Ona and Alice, he greeted Ona with a slight tip of the hat. The gesture was formal and stiff, suggesting the two weren't on the best of terms. Then he glanced at Alice and stopped, his face lighting up.

"Why, hello. I almost didn't recognize you out of a wedding dress. I'm Jeff MacDonald, owner of Old MacDonald's Realty and the mayor of Blithedale." He took Alice's hand and gave it a shake. "But then I already know who you are."

"Gossip travels fast in Blithedale."

"There's no denying it. But I also remember you from when you and your mother lived in Blithedale. I'm so pleased to see one of the Hartfords return to us."

He smiled, and even though she wanted to dislike him— after all, he opposed her friend's tiny house business—Alice couldn't help but return the smile.

"Plus," he said, "you've already made a good impression on my one employee, Kris Cox. She told me everything. And she sticks to the facts. So I got a favorable impression well before Todd Townsend could put his spin on the story."

He went on to talk about how Kris had gushed about Alice's integrity in the face of Chief Jimbo's spinelessness. "Don't think for a minute we're fools in Blithedale," he continued. "We know the shortcomings of our chief of police. Heck, I'm the first to know my own shortcomings, and admit them, too. But despite all that, we have a warm, welcoming community. Blithedale is a great place to live year round, and in summer, we host thousands of tourists who come to hike and relax. We're proud of what we've got."

The atmosphere in the bar and the delicious cocktail made Alice inclined to agree.

"Ah, and there are my guests," Mayor MacDonald said. "Mr. and Mrs. Oriel—I promised them drinks tonight, and I'm crossing my fingers that they'll choose one of the many, many houses they've looked at so far." He grimaced. "Of course you heard about how they dropped the Blithedale Books deal."

Alice nodded. "I had hoped they would take over the store."

"It would've been for the best," Mayor MacDonald said. He sighed. "But business is business."

He bid them a goodnight and headed toward the Oriels.

"He seems—" Alice began, searching for the right word, aware of the chilly atmosphere between Ona and Mayor MacDonald.

"Nice?" Ona laughed. "Sure he is. Until you oppose him. Jeff MacDonald didn't establish a monopoly on real estate in Blithedale just by being nice."

Alice looked across at Mayor MacDonald, who was slapping Mr. Oriel on the back and laughing. He looked harmless.

But couldn't even the sweetest, most harmless person turn out to be dangerous?

CHAPTER 26

The next morning, Wednesday, Alice left the Pemberley Inn to head for breakfast at the diner. She wasn't hungover after the long night gabbing and drinking with Ona, but she did need a hearty breakfast to buck her up. She couldn't remember the last time she'd had such a fun evening out.

Coming out the gate by the statue of Old Mayor Townsend, she was dreaming of bacon, eggs, and crisp toast with melting butter on it, when she noticed a cluster of people down the street to the right. So, instead of turning left toward the diner, she headed down the sidewalk and crossed over the street to take a closer look.

In front of Blithedale Books, the tributes to Vince had grown. More flowers. A screwdriver with a paper heart plastered to its handle. Plus, a bonsai tree with beautiful white flowers and white ribbons tied around its minute branches.

A woman with platinum blonde hair and a fake, carroty tan was standing by the flowers, staring at the bonsai.

"It's beautiful," Alice said. "Did you—?"

"I did not," the woman snapped, and Alice noticed that,

around her neck, she wore a gold chain. A gold chain with three heart pendants.

Before Alice could get a closer look, the woman bent down, grabbed the bonsai, and lifted it off the ground. Walking away, she held it with the tips of her fingers, as if she'd picked up something dirty, a bag of dog poo or roadkill. Reaching the nearest public trash can, she dumped the bonsai and wiped off her hands.

Then she glared at Alice.

"You got a problem with that?"

Alice shook her head, shocked into silence.

"Good," the woman said, dug out a pack of cigarettes from her pocket and lit one. Then she swiveled around and stormed off, leaving a trail of smoke in her wake.

For a moment, Alice stood still, not knowing what to make of the encounter.

"Typical," a voice said behind her. She turned and saw Bunce frowning at the arrangement of flowers. "People think they can dump flowers anywhere they like."

"Did you see that?" she asked him. "Did you see that woman?"

Bunce looked up and squinted at the woman in the distance.

"Mrs. Malone," he said. "She could at least have had the decency to throw out the rest of the flowers while she was at it."

But she didn't. She only threw out a bonsai tree.

Alice gazed after the woman—Vince Malone's widow—who was wearing a gold necklace with three heart pendants.

Alice decided she didn't want eggs and toast, after all. This morning, she was going to eat pie for breakfast.

CHAPTER 27

*B*onsai & Pie did good business in the morning. The line was long. As Alice sipped her coffee and chewed heavenly mouthfuls of egg-and-bacon pie, she watched Andrea box up one pie after another.

A truck driver in a baseball cap ordered the breakfast special, chatting with Andrea about the weather as Alice speared another piece of pie and savored the creamy egg and burst of salty bacon. The next customer in line was a woman with a loud voice who explained that she had no qualms about eating cherry pie for breakfast. She hurried out with her pie box and a grin on her face.

While Alice waited for a chance to talk to Andrea, she glanced at a cork board on the wall. Notices stuck to the board advertised private guitar lessons, yoga classes, and guided hikes through the woods. There was also a watercolor sketch of a cabin in the woods, the initials AC in the bottom right-hand corner.

But it was a newspaper clipping that caught her interest.

The paper cutout was not from *The Blithedale Record*, since that newspaper was online only. Its headline said, "David beats

Goliath: Local citizens stop high-profile development project."
The article mentioned Townsend Development's plan to build
a strip mall at the edge of Blithedale. But protesters had
stopped the bulldozers from breaking ground, and then, under
threat of legal challenge, Darrell Townsend backed down.

The photograph accompanying the article showed
protesters forming a human chain. Alice recognized several
people in the photo, each named in the caption: Kristin Cox,
Ona Rodriguez, and—standing front and center—Andrea
Connor.

Alice's heart skipped a beat. She leaned closer. Yes,
although the photo was grainy, it seemed Andrea was
wearing a necklace. A gold chain with a heart pendant.

"We're proud of that moment," she heard Andrea say
behind her, and Alice jumped.

Andrea wore a low-cut neckline revealing her collarbone.
It was bare. She wore no necklace. Where had her necklace
gone?

"Are you all right?" Andrea asked, concern on her face.

Thinking about what she saw, Alice realized, she'd put a
hand to her throat.

"I'm fine," she said, dropping her hand. Then added, "You
surprised me, that's all."

Andrea motioned to the newspaper clipping. "We stopped
Darrell Townsend that time. We won the battle. But I'm
afraid he'll win the war."

"What—?" Alice struggled to keep her gaze from falling
on Andrea's bare neck. "What do you mean?"

"Some of us fear Darrell's plans will destroy this town. I
heard the Oriels pulled out of the bookstore deal. Honestly, I
couldn't believe it when I first heard it."

"Because the deal was almost done?"

"That—plus the Oriels seem so committed to Blithedale.

They used to own a cabin in the woods, and now that they'd retired, they told me, they wanted to start a new life here. They were willing to overlook how run-down the bookstore had become. Other buyers won't. And that leaves Bunce with no choice. It's only a matter of time before Darrell talks him into selling."

Alice nodded. She didn't tell Andrea what she'd overheard —that Darrell had already gotten to Bunce.

Andrea said, "Of course, if someone could convince Bunce to fix that place up..." She shook her head. "But his idea of fixing things is slapping some spackle on the ceiling to keep the roof from caving in."

A customer came into the cafe and Andrea returned to stand behind the counter. While she boxed up a pie for the customer, Alice studied her.

As far as Alice knew, Andrea had no connection to the bookstore. But she had left a beautiful bonsai in tribute to Vince.

What had Esther said about Vince buying necklaces? He'd bought several, and always with a heart pendant. Like the one Andrea had been wearing when the newspaper photographed her at the protest. Or like Vince's wife, who wore three heart pendants on her necklace.

Darrell had seemed the most obvious suspect, because of his interest in the bookstore. His motive in killing Vince would have been to shut down the store and scare off potential buyers.

But what if the motive wasn't greed, but love? What if the killer pushed Vince, not because of the bookstore, but because he'd broken his lover's heart?

Andrea thanked the customer, and Alice's eyes dropped to the bare spot where a necklace ought to have been. Where the heart ought to have been.

Andrea put a hand to her chest. "What are you looking at?"

Alice snapped out of her reverie. "Uh, nothing…"

"Did I spill something?" Andrea looked down at herself—then up at Alice. She frowned. "What? You look like you've seen a ghost."

Alice tried to smile, aware that she looked like she was suffering from lockjaw. She'd never thought facing a murder suspect would make her knees turn to jello. What kind of detective crumbled at a moment like this?

She swallowed, and when she spoke her voice squeaked. "Andrea…"

Andrea touched Alice's shoulder. "You sure you're OK?"

"Vince…" She didn't get further. Andrea drew back her hand as if Alice's shoulder was a hot coal, and her eyes widened.

Alice said, "How did you know Vince?"

Andrea stared at her. Her face gradually cleared of emotion. It hardened. She said, "I didn't know Vince. I didn't know him at all."

Then she turned her back on Alice.

CHAPTER 28

*A*lice had an idea: If she could sneak into the bookstore and find the missing pendant, maybe she could prove Andrea killed Vince. Or, she whispered to herself, disprove it—and somehow discover how Darrell Townsend had masterminded the whole thing.

Once she got to the bookstore, though, Main Street was too busy—she couldn't sneak into Blithedale Books through the front door.

Behind the bookstore, she found a back door. Chief Jimbo had remembered to put a cease-and-desist notice on that, too. His book must've covered that procedure.

Unfortunately, the key she'd gotten from Becca didn't fit the lock. So she tried the door handle, hoping it was unlocked. It was a metal door, badly rusted, and as she yanked the handle, flecks of red fell to the ground. Mortar came loose from the brick wall around the doorframe. But it wouldn't budge. It was locked. Maybe even bolted on the inside.

She gave up, circling the bookstore and returning to Main Street. As she came around the building, she stopped.

Across the street, Andrea was striding down the sidewalk. She wore hiking boots and a backpack on her back, and she had the hunted expression of someone fleeing.

She's closed her cafe. She's bolting.

Alice stood rooted to the ground, unsure what she should do. In books, the heroes would pursue the suspect. But judging by Andrea's outfit, she was heading into the forest. And if she was the killer, Alice couldn't follow her into the Blithedale Woods alone.

Alice made a decision. It was time to do this by the book.

She came panting into the diner, having sprinted down the street.

"Chief Jimbo," she called out. She found him at a booth in the back. His book lay open on the formica table and he was studying it with a look of intense concentration, chewing the end of a pencil.

Breathlessly, she explained the situation. The necklace she'd found. The photo in Bonsai & Pie. Andrea's reaction to being asked about Vince. "And now she's running away."

Chief Jimbo took the pencil out of his mouth. He looked thoughtful. Then said, "Either that or she's going for a hike."

"In the middle of the day? When her business ought to be open?"

"Oh, in Blithedale, people close their businesses all the time to go fishing or hiking. Sometimes you need to clear your mind, you know."

Alice wanted to stomp her feet. He wasn't listening.

"But the evidence…"

Chief Jimbo cocked his head. "Tell me again about this necklace. How did you find it?"

"I found it—"

She stopped. She realized what she was about to do. She was about to admit to entering the bookstore illegally and snooping around. Chief Jimbo, she guessed, was more likely to take that offense more seriously than anything she'd said so far.

"Never mind," she said.

Chief Jimbo pointed his pencil at her. "You know, you might benefit from a hike in the woods, too. It's good for your mental wellbeing. It's true" He nodded at his own sage advice. "I read it in a book."

CHAPTER 29

fter her failure to enlist Chief Jimbo's help, Alice didn't know what to do. She ate a sandwich for lunch, barely tasting the ham and cheese on rye. Then sat at the diner counter, turning a spoon in a cup and staring down at the dredges of black coffee.

Becca, standing behind the counter, refilled her cup.

"Why so glum?" she asked.

Alice explained what she'd learned about Darrell Townsend and his dollar pendant. Then the bonsai with the white flowers that Susan Malone dumped in the trash—and the gold chain with three heart pendants.

"Oh, that?" Becca chuckled. "She used to have just one heart, but over time she's added to it. I bet it's got something to do with Vince."

It made sense. Everything about the heart pendants led back to Vince. Which brought Alice to why she was feeling to down. She told Becca about the photo she'd seen at Bonsai & Pie in which Andrea wore the necklace—and how the chief of police didn't take Alice's concerns seriously.

"Chief Jimbo didn't even react when I told him she was fleeing town. He said she must be going for a hike."

She'd expected outrage from Becca. Instead she got a shrug. "Maybe, for once, he's right."

"But Andrea's the most likely suspect…"

"And whenever someone puts on hiking boots and heads for the woods, what's the most likely explanation? If Andrea had been fleeing town, she wouldn't escape on foot."

Alice sighed. She put down the spoon and took a sip of coffee.

"Anyway, I feel terrible about the whole thing."

"And why is that?"

"Honestly, I had my heart set on Darrell Townsend."

"Because he's the big bad wolf?" Becca laughed. "He may not have murdered Vince, but that doesn't mean Darrell is innocent. You're right to look into Andrea's relationship to Vince, though. There's something there."

"But Andrea," Alice said with a sigh, "is so nice."

Becca nodded. "Well, you know what Mr. Jaggers tells Pip in *Great Expectations*?"

Alice didn't.

"'Take nothing on its looks,'" Becca said. "'Take everything on evidence. There's no better rule.'"

"You're saying Andrea isn't guilty until we know more."

"That's exactly what I'm saying." Becca winked. "It's what your mom would've said, too."

"I keep meaning to ask you—which mysteries did my mom get involved in?"

Becca shrugged. "Which ones *didn't* she get involved in? She investigated the ghost in the old Townsend mansion, and revealed that it was only Mad Dog Murray getting a kick out of scaring everyone. She solved the mystery of the missing marquee letters, helping the Bowers family recover their signage for the theater. And—most importantly—she helped my grandmother catch the thief who threatened to bankrupt the diner."

"Wait, someone tried to—"

Becca smiled. "That's a longer story for another time. My point is, you've got the Hartford sleuthing gene. Now, what's the next step?"

Alice sipped her coffee, thinking. She forced herself to calm down and put her thoughts in order. She considered the next step. Becca was right about suspecting Andrea—suspicion wasn't the same as proof. And she hadn't followed up on every clue that had come her way. Or every person involved.

"Everything leads back to Vince and those necklaces," she said. "And there's one person who must know more about Vince than anyone else. And she wears a necklace."

Becca smiled. "And I can tell you where she lives."

CHAPTER 30

The Malones' home was a modest ranch-style house among a row of equally modest ranches. Most houses had kids' toys scattered in the front yard. Swing sets. Abandoned frisbees. Tricycles dappled with rust. What set the Malones' place apart was the absence of toys. Plus the presence of a bright red convertible sports car in the driveway.

The convertible wasn't what she'd expected either Susan or Vince Malone to drive. Was this the right address? She checked the street and house number Becca had given her. It was the right house, all right.

Alice approached the front door and hesitated. Becca had told her that Susan and Vince had been a couple since high school, and it was an open secret that Vince had been unfaithful for most of their marriage.

It couldn't have been easy living with Vince, knowing he was unfaithful again and again. Hadn't Susan felt trapped? Alice couldn't help but think of her own situation.

If she'd wound up married to Rich she would have felt trapped. They wouldn't have been happy. She knew that. But after years of unhappiness, would they have cheated on each other? She couldn't imagine doing it, and it depressed her to think that she might never have left Rich or even tried to find joy elsewhere.

She shuddered. Thankfully, she'd dodged that bullet.

The question on her mind was why Susan hadn't dodged the bullet—and why she'd stuck with Vince, even after he'd wounded her again and again.

Alice rang the doorbell and waited. The door swung open.

Susan wore a tank top and a pair of pink sweat pants. Alice at once noticed the gold chain around her neck with three heart pendants. The fake tan couldn't hide Susan's deep crow's feet, nor the dark circles under her eyes. A cigarette smoldered in her right hand. She raised it to her lips and took a drag, eyeing Alice with undisguised disgust.

"So the runaway bride's come to throw a pity party for the widow, is that it?"

Alice got straight to the point. "I don't think Vince's death was an accident, and I want to find out who killed him."

If the news came as a shock to Susan, she bore it well. She inhaled and puffed out a cloud of smoke, her eyes as steely as before.

Then the fight went out of them and she sighed.

"You want coffee?"

Susan didn't wait for an answer. She turned her back on Alice and walked down the hallway. Alice closed the front door behind her.

The short hallway passed a living room in which a massive flatscreen TV covered one wall. Alice found Susan in the kitchen measuring spoonfuls of instant coffee into two cups. The electric kettle was hissing as it boiled water. Her stubbed-out cigarette, crushed into an ashtray on the counter, sent a dying line of smoke up toward the low ceiling.

"Milk? Sugar?"

"Black is fine."

"It's the only way," Susan said. "In my line of work, I see people pour all kinds of crap into their coffee, and I can't stand it. Coffee tastes good. Why the hell do you have to load it with syrup? If you want sweet, order a goddamn hot chocolate."

The kettle clicked off and she poured hot water into the cups.

In spite of the small kitchen, all the appliances looked not only new but high end. There was even an espresso machine —the same pro model Rich had bought for his kitchen. Alice knew little about espresso machines (though Rich could talk about them for hours), apart from the fact that this one was one of the most expensive.

Susan saw Alice looking at the machine.

"Fancy, isn't it?" Susan handed Alice her cup of instant coffee. "Vince thought it was cool. Personally, I still prefer instant. Or good old-fashioned drip coffee."

She led Alice through a sliding door to a back porch with two deck chairs.

The yard was long and narrow, and dominated by a large hot tub. Golden afternoon light slanted through the trees at the back.

Once they'd sat down, Susan said, "I was at the diner when Vince died. I didn't kill him."

She was so surprised by Susan's directness that Alice choked on her mouthful of coffee, triggering a coughing fit.

Susan gave her a hefty wallop on the back.

"Don't die on me," she rasped. "One sudden death is enough for me."

"I'm fine," Alice said.

"That's what you were wondering, though, wasn't it? Poor wifey has enough of cheating bastard, and so she pushes him off the scaffolding." She took a sip of coffee. "God knows there were times I was tempted."

Alice hesitated. Then took advantage of Susan's directness. "Well, why didn't you?"

"Kill him? Hell, I don't know. It's not my style, I guess. I can scream the head off the toughest, meanest trucker causing trouble at the diner, but violence disgusts me. No, I mean it: It makes me sick to my stomach. When people torture other people on TV, I turn it off. Give me something cozy on the Hallmark Channel any day of the week."

"What about the women he was with? Did you know them?"

Susan frowned. "I knew some of them. I could guess by the way they fell all over him. Like that stupid cow who owns that Bonsai & Pie place…" A smile crept across her face. "She had her fun with Vince, but in the end, I won. In the end, I always win."

"You won?"

"Sure. Whenever I threatened Vince with separation or divorce, he'd clean up. He'd drop the chick so hard she wouldn't know what hit her. That was what happened with that Andrea girl. He dumped her and came back home to me, back to being the Romeo he used to be in high school. He gave me another heart for my necklace."

She touched her necklace, fingering one of the three pendants, and let out a long sigh.

"One for Sally, one for Harriet, and lastly, one for Andrea. With each one, I'd allow myself to believe, you know, that maybe this time it would be different. It never was."

Even if, as Susan herself said, she won in the end, it wasn't much of a victory. She'd sacrificed so much to keep her marriage from falling apart. If Vince hadn't died, how many heart pendants would he have given Susan over the years?

"It sounds—" Alice spoke softly. "—so hard."

Susan dug into the pocket of her sweat pants for a pack of cigarettes. She pulled one out and turned it in her hand, considering it.

"Quitting Vince was like quitting cigarettes. I knew he was bad for me. Half the time I didn't enjoy our time together. But when he was good, aw man, he was *so* good. I guess I was always chasing those moments when it was best."

Susan lapsed into silence. Then lit her cigarette.

Alice nodded, more to herself than to Susan, who was gazing off into the distance.

Once again, she couldn't help layering her own experience onto Susan's. Why hadn't she torn herself free from Rich sooner? Why had it taken a trip down the church aisle for her to see the light?

But she'd been comfortable with Rich. She loved working at Crawley Books, and when he showed interest in her, the validation felt so good, it was easy to pretend that it was love. The week he'd promoted her to manager, Rich had asked her out on their first date. Looking back, it should've been a warning sign.

Alice considered the hot tub in the backyard. She thought of the shiny espresso machine in the kitchen, the giant flatscreen TV, and the sports car. Maybe Susan had been trapped by the many creature comforts.

"Vince liked nice things, didn't he?"

Susan glanced over at her. Then looked away, returning to her daydream. "Who doesn't?"

"But he must have spent a lot of money on this hot tub and the car and—"

"I see what you're getting at. That working people can't have nice things."

"That's not what I said. It's just that—"

Susan got to her feet, forcing Alice to do the same.

"It's exactly what you said, and I don't appreciate some fancy rich girl telling me what I can and can't have in my home."

"Rich girl?"

"I heard about that Vera Wang dress of yours."

"That was a knockoff, and honestly, I was only thinking that—"

Susan grabbed Alice's cup, yanking it out of her hand.

"Out."

"Hey, I didn't mean to—"

"Out."

Susan moved toward Alice, and like a dog herding sheep, Susan soon had her tripping down the hallway toward the front door.

On the front door step, Alice turned to apologize again and explain herself. But before she could say a word, Susan slammed the door so hard that the nearby living room window rattled.

Alice was left standing on the front step feeling stunned. What had happened? After their frank conversation, why had Susan's mood shifted so suddenly?

CHAPTER 31

"*I*f Vince dumped Andrea," Alice was explaining to Becca as the owner of the diner poured her another glass of ice tea at the counter, "then that might give her a motive for murder. But what about Sally and Harriet, his previous lovers?"

"Sally was a graduate student who stayed in Blithedale for a summer," Becca said. "Harriet moved across country with her husband. Both are long gone."

"What if one of them came back?"

Becca shrugged. "No one's seen either since they left. Why come back and take revenge on Vince now?"

"Good point. Andrea seems the most likely suspect." Alice sighed. "Then why did I come away from talking to Susan with the feeling that she was the guilty one?"

"Grief makes people say and do strange things."

"No, it was more than that, Becca. It was a sore point."

The walk back to Main Street had given Alice plenty of time to think it over. Once she got over the shock of being expelled, she shoved aside her fear that she'd offended Susan.

She didn't believe it. Susan had been frank and unflappable before that. There must be a big reason for her touchiness.

The dinner crowd had kept Becca busy, and Alice had helped her serve customers. Now things were quieting down and Alice felt her own hunger gnaw at her. She'd messaged Ona, asking if she wanted to join her for dinner at the What the Dickens, and every now and then she checked her phone to see if her new friend had responded. Sometimes making a new friend was as nerve-racking as dating.

Meanwhile, she sat at the end of the diner counter, chatting with Becca about her visit to Susan's.

"The sports car, espresso machine, hot tub," Alice said, counting off the items on her fingers. "If Vince and Susan had saved their money and paid for them—or they'd taken out bad loans to do it—then Susan wouldn't have gotten so defensive. But she was acting as if I'd accused her of doing something wrong."

Becca looked thoughtful. "I did always wonder where Vince got the money to buy those things."

"Unless Susan bought them."

Becca shook her head. "No. Susan doesn't have the money —or the interest."

Alice remembered what Susan had said about the espresso machine and preferring instant coffee. "She'd be happy with less, wouldn't she?"

"That's right. But Vince was the kind of guy who always had big plans. Big dreams."

"Did he do well as a contractor?"

"He did all right. It's not like we have a lot to choose from here in Blithedale. So he never lacked work. Though he did go through a rough patch some years ago—after an accident."

"What accident?"

"A cabin he worked on collapsed. It was in the local news. There were accusations of shoddy work, and it put some people off hiring Vince for a while. But time passed, and people forgot."

"What did people forget?" someone said behind Alice, and she turned on her stool and saw Ona come to the counter. Alice beamed. She was thrilled to see Ona. A giddy tickle rose from her stomach into her chest, like champagne bubbles. They'd had a blast at the Woodlander Bar, and Ona choosing to join her at the diner was a sign that, maybe, just maybe, they were becoming friends. Alice could use a good friend.

Ona sat down next to Alice and they both looked at the menu, trying to decide what to order. In the end, Ona ordered the burger and fries ("I finished another tiny house today...I could eat a horse") and Alice opted for the Cobb salad with grilled chicken.

Becca promised to join them.

"I've been dreaming about lasagna all day," she said.

As Becca moved off to get the food, Alice filled Ona in on the latest, trying to make it sound as if they were exchanging gossip, nothing more.

"So, Becca and I were talking about Vince and the cabin that collapsed."

Ona winked at her. "You mean, you were talking about your sleuthing, eh, Miss Marple?"

Alice felt the heat rise to her face. "I thought I was being subtle."

Ona laughed. Her laughter sparkled, the perfect complement to her rhinestone eyepatch. "You got pretty chatty at the Woodlander Bar. Plus, your sudden interest in what people are doing in Blithedale is a little unusual."

Ona laughed even more. Alice couldn't stay embarrassed —Ona's laugh was too contagious. She broke down, laughing just as hard as her friend.

"So, tell me," Ona said, "have you already solved the mystery of Old Mayor Townsend's missing journal?"

Alice shook her head. "No idea what that's about. I'm focused on who killed Vince Malone."

Ona gave Alice a playful nudge. "You don't pick the easiest mysteries, do you?"

She filled Ona in on her investigations, ending on her discovery that Andrea had fled town and that Susan Malone was hiding something.

Ona frowned. "That does seem strange…"

"And that's not all."

She told Ona about how Darrell Townsend had guessed she was snooping around his business, and that he threatened her.

"What did he threaten to do?"

"He said he'd—" Alice hesitated.

She liked Ona. She wanted to trust her. But she was reluctant to share details about Rich with anyone.

Ona put a hand on her arm. "It's OK. You don't have to tell me. I can guess. Darrell found out who you're running from, and he threatened to reveal that you're here in Blithedale."

"Yes." Alice let out a breath she didn't even know she was holding.

"Not surprising he'd do that. He's a slime ball."

"He seems to get what he wants."

She told Ona about her conversation with Andrea, and how Andrea had said the protesters had won the battle, but Darrell would win the war.

"She's right," Ona said. "The Oriels were a godsend for the bookstore. Now Bunce has made the situation impossible, playing right into Darrell's hands."

Alice rested her chin in her hands, her elbows on the countertop. "Andrea was right about this: If only Bunce bothered to invest in renovations, maybe he'd attract a different buyer."

Becca arrived with Ona's burger and fries.

"You know, crazy as it sounds, I sympathize with Bunce," Ona said, taking a big bite out of her burger.

"You do?" Alice said.

Ona nodded, chewing. Then said, "I'm not saying he's handled his side of things well. But he's clearly in over his head. It isn't easy running a business and owning the building. When I bought the Pemberley Inn, it was in a shambles. I didn't have enough money to fix the place up. Not the way I wanted. And no bank would give me a loan."

"But the inn looks beautiful."

"I did a lot of work. And I funded it by running fundraisers, auctioning off Jane Austen merchandise, nights at the inn, even my own skills as a carpenter."

"That worked?" Alice asked, surprised.

"It worked like a charm."

Ona's idea set off a chain reaction in Alice's mind. What if they could repeat Ona's success? What if they could raise money for Bunce, fix up the bookstore, and attract the right kind of buyers? Maybe they could convince Bunce to reconsider his deal with Darrell, after all.

"What you did to raise funds for Pemberley Inn," she said, "couldn't we do the same for the bookstore?"

"Do what Bunce should've done years ago?" Ona considered it, and then gave a shrug. "It might work."

"Of course it'll work," Becca said, leaning over the counter with a conspiratorial smile on her face. "And if we can convince Mayor MacDonald that this will lead to a more lucrative sale of the bookstore, plus keep downtown Blithedale safe from Darrell's bulldozers, I bet he'll force Chief Jimbo to lift the cease and desist order."

"Mayor MacDonald is all about business," Ona said, nodding. "His business."

Alice grinned. "Sounds like we have a plan. Who's in?"

"I'm in," Ona said.

"Me too," Becca said.

Alice felt her heart lifting with renewed hope. This might be a way to save the bookstore. Together, they could make this work.

"There's only one problem," Becca said, her smile faltering.

"What's that?"

"Bunce."

CHAPTER 32

$\mathcal{T}$he next morning, Thursday, Bunce sat in the diner booth facing Alice, his arms crossed, his frown deeper than usual as he listened to Alice lay out the plan.

Ona sat next to her. Having the inn-keeper at her side made Alice feel more confident. So did their other guest: Across from them, next to Bunce, sat Mayor MacDonald.

It had been a big win to get him to support their plan. Not only had he liked the idea, he'd offered to join them, in case he could help sway Bunce. But he wasn't optimistic. He warned them that changing the bookstore owner's mind was like trying to reason with a goat.

She finished presenting their fundraising idea to Bunce. They sat in silence, waiting for him to speak.

He didn't. He went on frowning at her.

"So, what do you think of the idea?" Alice asked.

Bunce snorted.

Alice glanced at Ona, who raised a shoulder in a shrug.

"You don't like it?" Alice asked Bunce.

"I hate it."

"All right." Alice took a deep breath and let out a sigh. "What part of it don't you like?"

"All of it," Bunce said. "Any of it."

"Because...?"

"Because you're expecting me to do all kinds of work." He said the word work as if it were something offensive, even perverse. "Ever since I bought the damn bookstore, it's been nothing but work, work, work. I'm done."

"But we're not asking you to do much..."

"There it is." He pointed an accusatory finger at her. "Those two pernicious words, 'not much.' I know how much work is involved in 'not much,' and I refuse to do it."

Mayor MacDonald said, "Bunce, you've never been much of a worker bee, have you?"

Bunce snorted again.

"I see," Alice said.

"I doubt you see anything," Bunce grumbled. "But at least now you know."

"Look, we're happy to do the work," Ona cut in. "Aren't we, Alice?"

Alice nodded. "We'll do the work. We'll even do it out of sight and out of earshot, if that helps."

Bunce narrowed his eyes, studying them with suspicion. "All of it?"

"All of it," Ona confirmed.

Bunce stared at them. Then shook his head.

"No. I know how it will be. I'll still end up being inconvenienced."

Mayor MacDonald sighed. "I'm afraid I was right. Bunce is, if nothing else, admirably committed to his stubbornness."

Becca came over to pour coffee refills. As she busied herself with filling coffees, she made a casual comment: "Bet there's one person who'll be much more inconvenienced."

Bunce glared at her. "Who? Who could possibly be more inconvenienced than me?"

"Darrell Townsend." Becca finished filling the cups and stood back. She gave a shrug. "What happens when the bookstore deal falls through? He already has plans for that space. He's probably scheduled bulldozers and the whole nine yards. All of it will have to be canceled. It will be a huge hassle. He'll be furious."

Bunce released his arms from across his chest and snatched up his cup of coffee and slurped it.

"How huge a hassle?" he asked, eyeing Becca with suspicion. "How furious?"

"Remember after that protest got in the newspapers and he had to abandon his strip-mall project? Remember how he smashed a window at his office?"

"Threw a chair right through it," Bunce said, and smirked.

Becca moved on to the next booth to refill someone else's coffee. Meanwhile, Bunce sipped his own coffee, his brows deeply furrowed as he thought. But the smile continued to twitch at the corner of his lips.

"All the money from the fundraiser goes to me?"

"To fix up the bookstore, so you can sell it."

"And you do all the work?"

"All the work," Alice said. "We'll raise the money by hosting an event and selling off your stock. Then we'll organize the refurbishments and work with Mayor MacDonald and Kris Cox to get new buyers. We'll do everything."

Bunce stroked his chin. Then leaned forward and said, "It's a deal, but—" He held up a finger. "—I'm not getting any younger while you all dilly-dally. I give you three days, until Saturday, to do this fundraiser. No more."

CHAPTER 33

*M*ayor MacDonald agreed to end the cease and desist order once the refurbishments began, but insisted the bookstore had to be closed for public safety. Chief Jimbo agreed. The decision to keep the store closed disappointed Alice, but Ona pointed out that it wasn't sensible to host a fundraiser in a building that was rumored to be unsafe. Better host it outside in the street and then, after the refurbishments, prove to all of Blithedale that the bookstore would stand for another hundred years.

Already that afternoon, they set up tables on the sidewalk outside the bookstore. Alice and Ona sold bargain books, served free lemonade, and handed out flyers for the big fundraiser party on Saturday.

While she mixed lemonade, Ona explained that Mayor MacDonald probably didn't mind supporting an event that might cause Darrell Townsend trouble either.

"Nobody likes Darrell," she said. "Even the mayor—whose realty business stands to benefit from some of Darrell's plans."

"But if no one likes Darrell, why do people tolerate him,

then? At the diner, so many people seemed to hang on every word he spoke."

"Is it any different with some of the big CEOs of billion dollar companies? People say they respect them. But deep down, they envy them. Or may even fear them. But whenever those powerful people speak out on an issue, folks pay attention."

"But why?"

"It's smart to stick close to the person with the most power. Some day Darrell may rule Blithedale, and when he's king, nobody wants him to remember them as his enemy."

"What about the people who've protested his projects? I saw you in that newspaper clipping—you were with Andrea and Kris at that protest."

Ona shrugged. "I'll worry about what King Darrell thinks when he puts on his crown. Until then, I'm going to fight him. This town is rough around the edges, but it's got soul. I don't want Blithedale to end up looking like a giant strip mall."

Esther, from the Love Again consignment store, stopped by for a lemonade, and the three of them chatted for a while. When Esther left, Ona excused herself. A guest had arrived at the inn and she dashed down the street to tend to her business, leaving Alice alone at the stand.

She handed out lemonade and flyers to people, including the Oriels.

Mr. Oriel, sipping his lemonade, said, "I'm impressed by your commitment. You must love this bookstore."

"I do," Alice said. "I want to make sure it's preserved."

He sighed. "I wish we could be the ones to do it."

"Not with that man haunting it," Mrs. Oriel said, putting down a book by John Irving she'd been considering. She picked up one by Joanna Trollope instead.

Alice, trying to be understanding, said, "The idea of a man dying there, must be off putting…"

"Oh, if it had been any other ghost," Mrs. Oriel said. "Or a dozen ghosts, for that matter. But the ghost of that man, Vince Malone." She grimaced. "I'll tell you—"

"My dear," Mr. Oriel cut in. "Let's not bore the young lady with our old tales of woe."

He raised an eyebrow, staring at his wife, as if wanting to convey an unspoken message. The message must've hit home, because Mrs. Oriel's eyes widened, and dropping everything about Vince Malone and ghosts, she paid for the Trollope and said, "Well, good luck with the fundraiser."

"But what were you going to say about Vince—?"

She didn't even have time to finish her question. The Oriels were hurrying down the street. Mr. Oriel had a hand on his wife's back, urging her onward. He glanced back once, an apologetic smile on his face.

What in the world, Alice wondered, was that about?

CHAPTER 34

When, later that night at the Woodlander Bar, Alice told Ona about her encounter with the Oriels, Ona shook her head. "They're an odd pair of ducks. But how could they be connected to Vince Malone?"

"Years ago, they spent their summers in Blithedale. They might have met Vince back then. But why would his ghost bother them?"

Ona said, "I love that you don't judge them for believing in the ghost. Most people would."

"Do you believe in ghosts?"

"Pemberley Inn has its ghosts. They don't bother me."

Alice recalled Mrs. Oriel's comment that "if it had been any other ghost." Ghosts didn't seem to bother Mrs. Oriel, either. So what was it about Vince that bothered the Oriels so much?

Half of Blithedale crowded the Woodlander Bar tonight, with every table occupied. When Alice went inside the tiny house to get another round of drinks, she admired how Thor moved behind the small bar, pouring gin from a jigger into a glass, adding ice, then tonic, and topping it off with a sprig of rosemary. Then, without missing a beat, he turned to the next drink.

When she'd wriggled her way to the bar, she ordered two glasses of Chardonnay, feeling good about giving him an easier task.

"It's hopping tonight," she said. "I can't believe how fast you can make those cocktails."

"Practice makes perfect," Thor said and popped the cork out of a wine bottle and poured two glasses.

"And with no one else in the bar to help you either," Alice added.

He handed her the wines and winked at her. "Sorry, I'm not hiring."

"Oh, no. I wasn't implying...I'm not even looking...I mean—"

She walked away with her glasses of wine, feeling flustered.

Back at the table, she handed Ona her glass, and Ona gave her a questioning look.

"You all right?"

Alice sat down and sipped her wine. She told Ona about her interaction with Thor, and as she described it, she realized her innocent comment about him having no help maybe hadn't been so innocent after all.

"Maybe I did kind of hope he'd ask if I would be interested in working here."

"He's a good-looking guy."

Alice swatted Ona on the shoulder. "It's not like that. I wasn't thinking about Thor—I was thinking of a job. I was thinking of staying."

"Staying in Blithedale?" Ona asked, and she leaned forward. "You should, you know? This is a great place."

Alice nodded. She would've loved to have worked at Blithedale Books with the Oriels as the owners. And maybe, if their plan succeeded, she'd still have a chance of landing a job at the bookstore. Still, the idea of getting a job, finding a place to stay, starting a new life was too daunting to wrap her mind around. She hadn't even figured out how to tie up loose ends with Rich.

She sighed. *Oh, Rich. I know we'll need to talk. Sooner or later.*

She wished she could put off the conversation forever.

Ona reached across the table and squeezed her hand. She seemed to understand.

"I know it's a lot right now. But think about it. You don't need to make a decision now."

"What do I know about bars, anyway?"

"Bookstores are your thing, aren't they?"

Alice gave Ona a sharp look. It seemed Ona could read her thoughts. Alice shrugged. "What does it matter? There's no bookstore job available…"

What if no bookstore job ever came her way? Could she find work at a place like this? She gazed around her at the Woodlander Bar, the tiny house Ona had built for Thor in its sylvan setting, the hurricane lights glowing at the edges of the clearing, the tables with candles, and all the people enjoying drinks.

She froze. Among the other patrons, she'd caught sight of Mrs. Oriel. Mr. Oriel joined her, placing two bottled beers on the table and sitting down. They must have arrived when Alice was inside getting drinks. She must have walked right past Mr. Oriel without seeing him by the bar.

The couple leaned close together. They were too far away —and the bar was too noisy—for Alice to listen in on their conversation, but from the way they sat close to each other, she guessed they were whispering. What was so important that they had to keep it secret?

Ona was right, the Oriels were a pair of odd ducks. But

they were also somehow wrapped up in this bookstore business, and Alice had a gut feeling that there was more to it than met the eye.

They had been excited about buying Blithedale Books and then pulled out after Vince's death. They would have known how run-down the store was. An accident shouldn't have changed their minds. They didn't even use it to pressure Bunce to drop the price. No, they wouldn't touch the building after Vince died, because of their belief in ghosts.

"The Oriels," Ona said. "What are they up to?"

"That's just what I was wondering."

They watched Mr. and Mrs. Oriel hunched together as if they were scheming.

Then their gestures became more animated, Mrs. Oriel's in particular. Mr. Oriel put a hand on his wife's shoulder. The gesture was tender. The look on his face was tender, too. And she reciprocated by putting a hand to his cheek.

Then they stood up and hurried toward the parking lot.

"Looks like they made some kind of decision," Ona said.

Alice felt a tug toward the parking lot. More than anything, she wanted to follow the Oriels and find out what they were up to. "I wonder where they're going," she said.

Ona drained her glass. "Only one way to find out."

Alice laughed. "You're the best, Ona."

CHAPTER 35

*W*ith Ona driving her pickup truck and Alice in the passenger seat, they followed the Oriels' burgundy Buick. The first surprise had been that the couple didn't turn toward the town center. Instead, they headed deeper into the Blithedale Woods.

Ona held back as far as she could. She drifted onto the shoulder to let an impatient driver in a Toyota Camry pass, putting the car between the pickup and the Oriels' Buick. After a while, the Camry revved its engine and, its tires screeching, shot into the oncoming lane to overtake the Oriels.

Tailing the Oriels was awkward. They drove at a snail's pace, and it seemed to Alice that the whole world, let alone the Oriels, must see that Ona's pickup was following them. Alice hugged herself. This detective stuff was nerve-racking.

For a while, the road rose and fell with the landscape, and then the Buick's brake lights flashed up ahead and the right-hand turn signal flashed and they turned onto a dirt road.

Ona slowed down. The pickup rolled past the entrance to the dirt road. In the distance, Alice saw the red taillights.

"Where are they going?"

"No idea," Ona said. "This is an old logging road. It's public land now, which, deeper into the woods, abuts private property."

She put the car in reverse, backed up, and then turned down the dirt road.

The pickup bounced on the potholed road. This would be rough terrain for the Oriels' sedan.

After 10 minutes, Alice saw taillights ahead. Ona saw them too, and she switched off the headlights.

"Let's see if we can sneak up," she said.

The pickup rumbled and rocked along the forest road. The woods were dark. Alice's eyes adjusted, but it was still a harrowing ride, the road growing dimmer and dimmer the deeper into the forest they went.

They turned a corner, and there it was, the Oriels' Buick. In the dark, the burgundy looked almost black.

Ona slowed the pickup truck and rolled closer. The Oriels had parked their car at the edge of the road. The car was empty. Alice squinted, trying to see farther into the woods.

"It looks like they've abandoned the car and walked from here."

"Then that's what we'll do, too," Ona said.

She drove ahead. The road curved, and fifty yards further into the woods, she pulled the pickup truck up to the trees and put it in park.

Then Alice and Ona backtracked to where the Oriels had parked their car.

"Which side of the road did they enter by?" Alice asked.

"The side they parked on?" Ona said. "That's what I would do."

"Fifty-fifty chance of success."

They stepped into the woods, and within moments, deep

darkness shrouded them. Alice tested the ground ahead of her, placing her feet with care. Rocks and sudden dips made the terrain perfect for twisting an ankle. She could see nothing up ahead, no sign of the Oriels, only the black trunks of trees against the dark-gray gloom of night.

Either the Oriels hadn't come this way or they were much further in. She dug out her phone to turn on her flashlight, and as her screen lit up—showing more missed calls and messages from Rich—she saw she had no reception. It made her stomach twist into a knot. How many movies had she seen where the hero lost cell phone reception right before encountering a crazed serial killer?

"No reception," she whispered to Ona, showing her phone.

Ona checked her phone and shook her head. "Same here. A lot of places in the woods get spotty reception, because of the valleys and gorges between the hills and mountains. In fact, we may be close to Dead Man's Gorge."

"Dead Man's Gorge? Really?"

Why couldn't people gives places nice names like Nice Neighborly Gorge or Cozy Canyon? Alice let out a sigh and stuffed her phone back into her pocket, continuing her careful trek through the dark.

The minutes ticked by. She was getting used to walking in the dark, growing more and more confident that she wouldn't twist her foot or fall. She was so intent on trying to see where she was stepping that she let out a little yelp when Ona grabbed her arm.

"Look," she whispered.

Up ahead, lights glowed among the trees. Alice got excited. Finally, they were going to find something. She picked up the pace. Her eyes locked on the lights ahead as she clambered around the giant trunk of a tree. She stepped from one big rock to another, then scrambled up a low ridge.

At the top of the ridge, the lights grew clearer. Long, glowing rectangles. Light spilling onto straight-edged forms.

"A house," she mumbled to herself.

She turned to Ona, who was trailing behind, and whispered, "There's a house."

It would take Ona some time to catch up. Alice couldn't wait. She wanted to see what this house was, and whether the Oriels might be inside.

She hurried forward, her eyes still locked onto the house, and her feet swiftly navigating roots and stones and treacherous dips. The house was all straight lines. Modern. With a deck jutting out into dark nothingness.

What is this place? A modern home in the middle of the woods?

She put down her right foot and found only air. Her body pivoted forward. Pitch blackness lay below, not the dark contours of rocks and earth that her eyes had grown used to, and she realized she was about to fall, and fall far.

She drew in sharp breath, a preamble to a scream, when hands gripped her from behind and yanked her back.

She fell. But she fell backward, slamming her butt down on a tangle of roots, and her scream turned into an "oof!"

Familiar faces emerged from the darkness.

Mr. and Mrs. Oriel stood over her, Mr. Oriel shaking his head. "You must have a death wish, young lady."

CHAPTER 36

"**I**f I hadn't grabbed you in time," Mrs. Oriel said, "you would have stepped right into the Dead Man's Gorge and taken a nasty tumble."

"Uh," Alice said, feeling dazed. "Thank you."

"You're welcome, dear," Mrs. Oriel said and patted her shoulder.

Ona joined them. "Is everyone all right?"

"Everyone's all right," Mr. Oriel said. "Now, mind telling us what you're doing hiking the woods in pitch darkness?"

Alice looked at Ona, who shrugged, then turned back to Mr. Oriel.

"We were following you. We wanted to know what *you* were doing hiking the woods in pitch darkness."

Mr. Oriel, sighing, turned to Mrs. Oriel. "See? I told you this skulking about would get us into trouble."

"We've done nothing wrong." Mrs. Oriel crossed her arms. "It's a free country. And this is public land. We can take a late night hike if we want."

Alice got to her feet and groaned, feeling the ache in her butt and on the backs of her thighs.

"It's got something to do with that house, doesn't it?"

Mr. and Mrs. Oriel exchanged meaningful glances.

"Who lives there?" Alice asked. "Anyone we know?"

"I can tell you that," Ona said. "That house belongs to none other than Darrell Townsend."

Ona's words sent a jolt through Alice. Of course. The modern house with its box-like shape and its unusual location—this was the kind of place she'd always imagined Darrell would live in.

"What's your connection to Darrell Townsend?" she asked the Oriels.

"Nothing," Mr. Oriel said.

Mrs. Oriel tugged at his sleeve. The couple conferred in whispers, and Alice caught Mr. Oriel saying, "All right, might as well..."

When they turned back to Alice and Ona, their standoffishness was gone. Mrs. Oriel had uncrossed her arms. Mr. Oriel cleared his throat.

"We have nothing to do with Darrell Townsend. But we do have something to do with the Dead Man's Gorge." He stared across the black gorge to the house perched on its side. "Over there was where we once had a cabin. Years ago, we used to come to Blithedale every summer. We loved it here. We lived in a suburb to the city, where our jobs were, but every year, we counted down the months, weeks, and days until we could visit the cabin."

He let out a long, weary sigh.

Mrs. Oriel picked up the story. "That cabin was the only place we'd ever felt at home. It was small and cozy. Perfect for the two of us. We planned to renovate it, bit by bit, to weather proof it and make it a year-round home. There was a deck that jutted out over the gorge, a more modest version of what Mr. Townsend has constructed over there. It wasn't safe, though. And although we can paint and do some basic repairs, we needed a contractor to help us fix it. We found one. A local guy."

"Let me guess," Alice said. "Vince Malone."

Mrs. Oriel grimaced. "That's right. Vince Malone. He gave us an excellent price and got to work. He was going to strengthen the integrity of the deck and then fix some floorboards inside the cabin, too. We left at the end of the summer, expecting Vince to finish the job during the fall."

She looked at her husband, her face drooping, her eyes turning glassy. He took her hand and held it.

"Vince screwed it up," Mr. Oriel said. "While working on the deck, the supports shifted, and the whole thing collapsed."

"Collapsed?" Alice drew in a sharp breath. "That's terrible."

"It gets worse. The deck destabilized the entire cabin, and within days, the house began sliding over the edge. The authorities deemed the cabin unsafe, and we had to pay for its removal. Only weeks before, I'd lost my job. Money was tight on one salary. By the time we paid for the removal of the cabin, we couldn't afford to rebuild. We couldn't even afford to hold on to the land."

"So you sold?"

Mr. Oriel nodded. "We had no choice, and despite our demands for an investigation into Vince's malpractice, nothing came of it. Nothing could be proven. We knew Vince's shoddy work destroyed our dream. We went to the local newspaper to tell our story, but the next day, we got a call from a lawyer, threatening us with a lawsuit. We couldn't afford to get involved in that kind of thing. So we gave up. We kept the truth to ourselves."

"But then you came back to Blithedale," Alice said.

Mrs. Oriel, tears gathered in her eyes, added, "We came back to try our luck once more. But when Vince Malone died, we knew he'd sabotaged our dreams again by haunting the bookstore. We couldn't stomach spending our days in a business where his spirit might linger."

"So, you see," Mr. Oriel continued, "we come here at night because of the place itself. It's like visiting the grave of a favorite relative. It's painful but also brings us peace and joy. Do you ever get that feeling from a place?"

Alice knew what he meant. Her place was Blithedale Books, and the little wardrobe with the red door. Though her mind also flashed on the Woodlander Bar and the What the Dickens Diner, fresh images of Becca and Ona mixing with her old childhood memories.

"We're excited to retire to Blithedale," he said. "We would like to continue to work, which was why the bookstore interested us. We remember what an oasis the bookstore used to be—before Mr. Bunce bought it—and we'd hoped to rekindle some of that magic. But more than anything, we want to recreate some of the happiness we felt at that old cabin."

Mr. Oriel put an arm around his wife and she leaned her head on his shoulder.

"I understand," Alice said, surprised by how emotional she felt. A lump grew in her chest, threatening to bring tears. Their story made her feel sorry for them. It also reminded her of her mom and the old bookstore. "We're sorry we stuck our noses in your business."

Mr. Oriel laughed. "We're sorry we were acting so suspicious."

Alice and Ona bid the Oriels a goodnight, and they were going to head back toward the pickup truck, when a thought occurred to Alice. She turned back to the Oriels.

"Did you at least get a good price for the land when you sold it?"

Mrs. Oriel shook her head. "The accident had scared off

potential buyers. Mr. Townsend, who had shown interest in our land even before the accident, offered us a low price. So low that, under other circumstances, it would've been insulting. But since he was the only one willing to buy, we were grateful."

Alice nodded. This story sounded so reminiscent of the sale of Blithedale Books. Vince's accident had ruined the sale prospects. In the end, Darrell Townsend would get what he wanted at a cheap price.

The whole situation stank to high heaven. And Alice couldn't forget what Darrell himself had said, "The law can bend so far, why bother breaking it?" The question was how far Darrell had bent the law.

CHAPTER 37

On Friday, Alice kept busy at the fundraiser stand. Ona had come dressed up in Regency period costume—one of her many Jane Austen-inspired outfits she'd collected over the years, she explained. This outfit consisted of a riding jacket over a white muslin gown.

"It's called a Spencer jacket." Ona twirled around, showing off. "Dashing, isn't it?"

Alice smiled. "You look great."

Ona relieved her for a lunch break, and Alice took the time to check on Bonsai & Pie. It was still closed. No one had heard from Andrea. But Chief Jimbo continued to insist that everything was all right.

But what if Andrea was the killer, and she'd skipped town?

Alice sold lots of books. By the time Saturday morning came, Bunce himself grudgingly admitted that she'd sold more books in a couple of days than he'd done all year.

"If you're so good at this, why don't you buy the book-store?" he grumbled.

"I can't afford it. My savings might cover the cost of

inventory, but buying the property and fixing it up...? No way."

He snorted, and as he shuffled off, he said, "Young people. No sense of financial planning."

Alice would've liked to point out that he himself didn't seem to know so much, since he'd run his business into the ground. But it wouldn't do any good antagonizing Bunce. Instead, she focused on her next customer, the next glass of lemonade, the next flyer for the fundraiser.

An SUV drifted down Main Street. The window rolled down, revealing Darrell Townsend inside in the driver's seat, his brother Todd next to him. She expected him to glare at her. After all, they were ruining his plans.

But Darrell smirked. It sent goosebumps down her arms. What did he know that she didn't? Why was he still so confident? He revved the engine and drove away.

Alice forced herself to forget about Darrell. She wouldn't let him sour their party. Especially not when things were going so well.

A bluegrass band, a local trio called the Pointed Firs, set up to play. One played a guitar, another a banjo, and the last a washboard. They were friends of Ona's and happy to play for free. Becca brought coffee urns and disposable cups. Kris joined Alice behind the stand, helping to serve customers.

"I love doing something for this town," she said. She leaned closer to Alice. "If we don't stop Townsend Development, he'll bulldoze the whole town."

"Let's make sure that doesn't happen."

"Go Team Blithedale!"

Kris grinned and gave Alice a thumbs up, then got back to handing out cups of coffee to guests.

The band played the old song "Shady Grove" while a throng of people gathered around the stand on the sidewalk, spilling into the street. Chief Jimbo arrived to put up barriers, reducing Main Street to single-lane traffic, which he directed.

People ate Becca's muffins and drank her coffee and browsed the books Alice put on display. The Oriels showed up and they greeted Alice with genuine warmth. Maybe sharing their secret had made them feel like Alice was halfway toward becoming a friend. It was funny how secrets affected people—a secret told could either create a bond or break it.

People around her laughed and talked. A couple of pre-teen sisters danced to the music, and their white-haired grandmother joined in.

Alice smiled. The festive mood was contagious. She watched people intending to pass the fundraiser, even walking past, then stopping to confer ("we've got time" and "sure, let's do it"), and coming back to the party.

When the bluegrass trio took a break, Ona got on a soapbox and cracked open a copy of *Pride & Prejudice* and began reading. It turned out that she was a natural at reading Austen's prose, including giving each character their own distinct tone of voice.

> "My dear Mr. Bennet," said his lady to him one day, "have you heard that Netherfield Park is let at last?"
>
> Mr. Bennet replied that he had not.
>
> "But it is," returned she; "for Mrs. Long has just been here, and she told me all about it."
>
> Mr. Bennet made no answer.
>
> "Do not you want to know who has taken it?" cried his wife, impatiently.
>
> "You want to tell me, and I have no objection to hearing it."

That got a laugh from the audience.

Nearly all eyes were riveted on Ona. Kris was busy with

the many people who wanted coffee and muffins. Alice had taken charge of selling books, and it had gone so well that the pile had dwindled.

An idea formed in her mind. She had an excuse to leave.

She found Bunce at the edge of the crowd, frowning up at Ona, his arms crossed on his chest. "I've never enjoyed Jane Austen," he complained. "But at least Ona knows how to read."

It was as close to a compliment as Bunce ever came. Even he was captivated by Ona's performance.

Alice explained that they were low on books.

"You go get them," Bunce snapped. "Remember the deal: You do the work. I'm busy watching this silly performance."

Completely engrossed, he was obviously unwilling to miss a moment of Ona's reading. Alice smiled to herself. Even Bunce wasn't immune to Ona's charm. Nor to Jane Austen's.

Alice turned on her heels, and touched her pocket to check that she still had the key Becca had given her, when Bunce called her name.

"Miss Hartford, aren't you forgetting something?"

"I am?"

He dangled a set of keys in front of her.

"Oh, yeah. Thanks."

Phew. That was close.

It would've been bad if Bunce had realized that she could get into the bookstore without his keys.

She unlocked the door to Blithedale Books and slipped into the gloomy interior.

The ramshackle shelves and dirty floor. The dust motes swirling in the air. The place looked so unchanged, it surprised Alice. So much had happened since she'd come to Blithedale, returning to the red door for the first time since childhood.

Did she have time to visit her hideaway?

Probably not.

But she would do it anyway.

She found the wardrobe with the red door exactly as she'd left it. She opened the door and it creaked. The whole thing shook. The cushions were as flat as ever, and *Alice's Adventures in Wonderland* still lay hidden underneath.

She sighed, clutching the book to her chest. She wished she could remove the wardrobe and take it with her. Yet she also knew that would never be enough. The wardrobe was her personal hideaway, but she could never sacrifice the rest of the bookshop—and judging by the initial success of the fundraiser, she might not have to. They would raise the money. They would help Bunce fix up the bookstore, sell it the Oriels or someone else, and ensure Blithedale Books returned to its former glory.

"Don't worry," she whispered, hoping whatever remained of her mom's spirit might hear her. "I won't let you go."

After a few minutes of sitting still, she heard the sound of the bluegrass band strike up another song. Her mind was too full of questions about Vince's death to fully concentrate. Later, she would find time for her hideaway. Then she'd experience once more that feeling of closeness with her mom. Later.

With a sigh, she got to her feet and replaced the book under the cushion and closed the red door again.

She moved among the bookshelves, picking out books they could sell at the stand. She focused on classics and popular fiction: *To Kill a Mockingbird* by Harper Lee, *Cannery Row* by John Steinbeck, *Gaudy Night* by Dorothy L. Sayers, *Are You There, God? It's Me Margaret* by Judy Blume, *Sweet Danger* by Margery Allingham, *Mrs. Dalloway* by Virginia Woolf, *Possession* by A.S. Byatt, *Great Expectations* by Charles Dickens, *Artists in Crime* by Ngaio Marsh, *Midnight's Children* by Salman Rushdie, *The Prime of Miss Jean Brodie* by Muriel Spark, and *The Count of Monte Cristo* by Alexander Dumas.

The pile of books got heavy.

That's enough. Now, let's see if that pendant's hiding back here...

Weaving in and out of the bookshelves, Alice found herself at the very back, standing at the foot of the scaffolding. She gazed upward. That was the cross-brace that had held the necklace. She looked down at the floor. Then over her shoulder.

How much time did she have to spare before someone noticed her absence?

She set down the pile of books. Scanning the floor, she focused on catching anything that reflected. If there had been a pendant on the necklace—the one Andrea might have worn —then it ought to have landed somewhere close to the feet of the scaffolding.

Bent over, she gazed at each linoleum tile. The clean ones, of course, had nothing on them at all. After the coroner removed Vince's body, someone cleaned the tiles, leaving no trace of his death.

The area close to the bookshelves revealed nothing. Nor did the area within the scaffolding. She'd almost given up, when she thought she caught a glint of gold near the wall.

The scaffolding beams pressed against the back wall. By one of these metal bars, right where it met the floor and the wall, the gold winked at her.

She knelt down. There was something there. But the metal scaffolding wedged it against the brick wall. She tried to free it, but without luck.

Looking up at the metal structure above her, she bit her lip. How easy would it be to move the scaffolding, even just a little? And was it safe? Presumably, it had been built to stand strong. Even if she nudged it, it shouldn't be a problem.

Should it?

She stood next to the scaffolding, and gripping the metal bars with both hands, she put all her strength into lifting and shoving it. Her knuckles scraped against the brick wall. The scaffolding moved a little.

She let out a breath of air and laughed, thrilled that her efforts were already working.

But it wasn't enough. When she bent down to check the pendant—she could see it was a pendant now—it was still too firmly lodged. One more shove...

She gripped the metal bar and gave it a big heave.

Yes!

The pendant rolled out from its hiding place.

Alice gave a whoop of joy.

She crouched down and picked up the pendant. A single gold heart.

That was when she heard the crack. It sounded as if someone was crushing a cracker underfoot. The scaffolding shook, and for a moment, she had the insane idea that the metal was all crumbling.

What's happening? Metal doesn't sound that way.

Then a brick fell from high above, striking one of the metal bars and breaking into pieces. A shower of dust followed by another brick. And then half a dozen hammered down on the scaffolding and the floor, an ear-deafening, clattering percussion.

She saw it, but she couldn't move, fear rooting her legs to the floor.

The wall...the ceiling...

It was coming down. Right on top of her.

CHAPTER 38

A brick struck the metal bars, cracked in two, and one half spun through the air and grazed Alice's shoulder. The pain woke her. She stumbled backward, a fiery urgency pumping through her veins and into every limb.

The wall made a grinding sound as it leaned toward her, crushing the top of the scaffolding. The metal structure came apart. Bars and braces snapped off each other. Some tumbled down—there was a thundering din as they hit the floor—even as the remaining scaffolding tipped toward Alice.

She spun around and ran. Something hard and sharp knocked into her back. A metal bar clattered down by her feet, catching her right foot. She jumped, untangling from it.

Then she was running through the aisle between two bookshelves, and as she glanced back over her shoulder, she saw the scaffolding fall toward her. She screamed. It would hit her. It would bury her.

The metal bars struck the tops of the shelves with a crack. Bricks broke against the scaffolding, sending splinters of rock at her, but the metal bars held back the worst of the wall.

She stumbled away just in time.

An enormous boom filled her ears. The noise drowned out everything else as bookshelves collapsed in on themselves, metal bars came loose, and bricks and mortar came crashing down in a huge pileup.

Then hands wrapped around her, and Alice looked down, seeing a pair of ruffled sleeves grasping her. Ona. Pulling her back, away from the giant cloud of dust that was billowing toward them.

Sunlight…the safety of the sidewalk…Alice on her hands and knees, coughing, and coughing, and coughing, feeling as if she might spit up her lungs.

"My God," she heard Becca say, her voice far away, "are you all right?"

A sharp thing dug into the palm of her right hand. She opened it and saw the heart pendant, the gold glinting in the sunlight.

Tears streamed down her face, and through blurry vision, she could see a forest of legs around her. Ona, crouched down next to her, had an arm around her.

She pulled Alice into a hug.

"You're safe now," she said.

Alice wanted to speak, drew in fresh air, but her voice failed her, and she had another coughing fit.

"Everyone back," Chief Jimbo was telling the crowd. "Everyone away from the store—it's not safe, it's not safe!"

Another crash, boom, and bang made the crowd cry out with surprise, and then a wave of dust rolled across the sidewalk.

"No…" she croaked, thinking of the bookstore she loved, the red door, and the memories of her mom. "No…"

CHAPTER 39

The bowl of steaming chicken soup smelled delicious, but Alice hadn't tasted it. She hadn't even touched the spoon by its side.

"Eat, please," Becca said, looking at Alice and then giving Ona, who sat next to Alice, a worried look. "You'll feel better."

Alice couldn't imagine that food would make a difference. Not at a time like this.

"We need to look at that wall," she said. Her voice was hoarse, and only a notch above a whisper. The dust from the collapsed wall and ceiling in the bookstore had wreaked havoc on her lungs and throat. "And the ceiling. The scaffolding must've held it in place. That was no accident…"

"All in good time," Becca said.

"There's no time. Before the evidence disappears, we have to get in there."

"We can't, Alice," Ona said. She was still wearing her Regency outfit, except it all looked gray, covered in mortar dust. "Chief Jimbo has cordoned off the area. The volunteer firefighters have gone over the structure, and they've confirmed the obvious: The bookstore building is too dangerous to enter. The rest of the ceiling could collapse at any moment."

"But it can still be fixed, right?" Alice looked at her friend. "We'll finish the fundraiser, we'll renovate, we'll find buyers…"

Ona took Alice's hand. "Sweetie, it's over. The fundraiser didn't work out."

"Didn't—?"

Alice was confused. "But we were selling books. There were so many people…"

Becca said, "The money we raised on book sales was good. But it would never be enough to fix the bookstore. Not now."

Kris slid into the booth, sitting next to Becca, across from Alice.

"Becca's right," she said. Her eyes were bloodshot, as if she'd been crying. "I spoke with Mayor MacDonald, and he says the building will be condemned. It's too unsafe."

"What?" Alice leaned forward, almost knocking her soup bowl over. "That can't be true. There must be a way to save the bookstore."

"Bunce doesn't believe there is," Kris said. "He says—"

Her eyes filled with tears, and she had to take a moment to recover before adding, "He says that he's going to sell to Darrell Townsend. That he doesn't have a choice. Darrell's the only one who will buy, and even then, it's such a low bid, Bunce might as well be giving it away for free."

Just like with the Oriels' cabin…

And once again, Darrell would win. He would count on everyone giving up once the building had collapsed. But Alice wouldn't give up.

I've got to save the red door…my Wonderland…and not just that…

When she'd first come to Blithedale, the wardrobe with the red door—her hideaway—had mattered the most. But she saw now that the joyful memories of her childhood lived on in the bookstore itself.

I've got to save Mom's bookstore...whatever's left of it.

Alice tried to stand, which wasn't possible in the confines of the booth, and turned to Ona, trying to shove her way past.

"We've got to talk to Bunce. We can raise more money. Offer a higher price. Buy the property before Darrell destroys it."

Ona put a hand on her shoulder.

"Alice," she said, her voice so low and slow, it was like a mother speaking to her child. "We tried. Becca, Kris, and I offered to pool our savings. Which isn't much. But it wouldn't amount to more than what Darrell's offering."

"No..."

Ona gently guided her back down to her seat. Alice slumped down, her whole body going limp as Ona's sad eyes told her what she knew deep down: They couldn't save the bookstore from destruction.

She leaned her elbows on the table and put her face in her hands.

Becca and Kris whispered about the situation, but the words blurred together in Alice's tired mind. Vaguely, she was aware of Becca and Kris leaving the booth. But Ona stayed, still holding her hand.

"There must be some way to save the bookstore..." Alice mumbled, her mind a confused muddle of clues and questions: *Darrell's plans...ceiling collapsing...gold necklace...Old Mayor Townsend's journal...Mom's bookstore...*

She shook her head, trying to clear her mind. She had to focus on the immediate problem: How to stop Bunce from selling to Darrell.

If only she knew someone who cared about bookstores enough to step in and offer Bunce a higher price. Someone who wouldn't raze the building to construct a strip mall. Someone whose passionate love for books would ensure Blithedale Books continued to exist as an independent bookstore...

She raised her head from her hands. A massive weight pressed down on her, a weariness that made her too exhausted to even cry. Because she knew who she'd just described.

Someone who cared so deeply about books that he'd step in to save an independent bookstore.

She dug out her phone.

"Alice, what are you doing?" Ona asked.

"I'm calling Rich."

CHAPTER 40

"*A*re you sure this is a good idea?" Ona asked after Alice explained why Rich was her only hope. Alice stared at her phone. She'd brought up Rich in her contacts. All she had to do was press "call."

"What choice do I have?"

"How can your ex-fiancé fix this?" Ona said. "Even if he could solve the problem, sweetie, why would he? You left him at the altar."

She spoke gently, but also truthfully. Her words did not sting Alice. After all, she'd asked herself the same questions. Yet she knew Rich. She knew what he'd do.

With a sigh, she said, "If I ask him to, he'll buy the bookstore."

"And what will he get in return?"

Alice looked away.

"Alice, listen. You ran away for a reason."

Alice said nothing. She was thinking of her hideaway behind the red door, her Wonderland, and the bookstore that held her happy childhood memories, the last remnant of her mom. It would all vanish if she didn't do something. But exhaustion rode over her in waves. She couldn't muster the strength to explain.

Ona must have taken her silence as promising, because she squeezed Alice's hand and said, "You should sleep on it. Come back to the inn with me, get some rest, and then we can grab breakfast and talk it over tomorrow."

Alice shook her head. "It'll be too late by then."

"Nonsense. Between now and the morning, all that will happen is that we'll get some sleep and a fresh perspective on things. Maybe we'll find a solution we haven't thought of."

Alice shrugged.

"I'll take that as a yes," Ona said.

She tugged Alice's hand and guided her, like a child, out of the booth, and then led her out of the diner.

Down the street, a firetruck stood by the bookstore. So did Chief Jimbo's police cruiser. Barriers kept people at a distance, and the chief of police was busy directing traffic. He'd sent word to the diner that he'd want to talk to Alice later to learn what happened, but that he had "other fish to fry first."

From afar, Alice could see the big, gaping hole in the back of the bookstore, where not only the wall, but also the roof had caved in.

She didn't comment. Nor did Ona.

They reached the Pemberley Inn, and Alice began climbing the steps to her room.

"Do you want some company?" Ona asked.

Alice shook her head. "I'm going to have a shower and go straight to bed."

"Good idea. I'll see you in the morning."

Ona gave her an encouraging smile.

Alice climbed the steps, her feet as heavy as bricks.

Colonel Brandon stared at her with those empty eyes, and she stared back.

"You'd come to my rescue, wouldn't you, Colonel Brandon?" She considered him for a moment. "Of course you would."

She went inside her room, closed the door, and sat on the bed.

Deep breath. Exhale.

She hit the call button.

CHAPTER 41

"*A*lice?"

Rich's voice, tentative, as if he might be mistaken, made Alice grip the phone hard. Elbows on her knees, she leaned forward, the phone pressed to her ear as she stared at the floor.

"It's me," she confirmed.

"Sweetheart, I've been so worried. Everyone has. But you're OK. You're all right?"

"I'm all right."

He let out a sigh. "What a relief. I walked the city, trying to find you, and then racked my brain for where you might be outside the city. And then there were the guests, of course. People who traveled for the wedding. I bought them all-day tourist passes and hosted a big dinner, and it seemed everyone had a delightful time. So you don't need to worry about them. They were fine. You must have been so lonely, though, and frightened. I mean, after you ran, I thought, my goodness, she's hurting. So I asked around about you and…"

As he spoke, voicing his concern for her, and everything he'd done to fix the mess she'd made, his soft voice, so full of concern and sympathy, made her head and limbs, not to mention her heart, feel heavy and dull. She closed her eyes, feeling sleepy. He had always been like this. Like the poppy field in *The Wonderful Wizard of Oz*, lulling poor Dorothy to sleep.

Becca and Ona no doubt thought she'd run from an abusive psychopath. But Rich was kind and attentive. He wouldn't hurt a fly. In fact, if he saw an ant on the sidewalk, he'd walk around it, careful not to step on it. His greatest pleasure was to please her, and he applied himself to this task with the intensity of someone training for a marathon.

There wasn't a moment he wasn't hovering over her, asking her if she needed something, bringing her baked goods or pillows or face cream—or any of the other things he thought might make her happy in the moment.

At first, she'd been amazed. It felt so good to be the center of attention. So loved and pampered.

For a while.

She moved into his apartment, and suddenly discovered that her crappy four-story walk-up studio had been the only place she could truly call her own. Now they lived together and worked together. They never spent time apart.

She asked him for some space—for a little alone time, a little headspace—and he'd complied by giving her a hand-made card for a spa. Except the spa was staffed by him, set up in their apartment, with scented candles everywhere, meditation sounds on the stereo, and three scheduled hours of massage and kombucha tea breaks. Not a minute to herself.

On the phone, his voice droned on and on and on. So familiar. Exactly as it had done at home and at work in the city. In her old life.

She snapped awake. No, she wouldn't get lulled by him again. Not yet. There was something she needed to accomplish first.

With her left hand, free from the phone, she grasped her left thigh and dug her fingernails into her flesh until it hurt. It helped a little. She sat up straight.

"Rich," she said, interrupting his endless, soporific stream of chatter. "I called because I need your help."

"Of course, sweetheart. Anything you need."

"I'm in a small town, and there's an independent bookstore here."

"Love it already, sounds like the perfect place to spend some time, wish I were there with you right now," Rich said, the words gushing out. Then, "Oh, sorry. Didn't mean to interrupt. Please go ahead."

"The bookstore's in trouble. The owner wants to sell. A wall has collapsed—part of the ceiling, too—and the place has been condemned."

"Oh."

"And a local developer wants to tear it down and build a parking lot."

"That's awful."

"I need you to buy the property and save the bookstore."

A reasonable human being would've had a hundred questions and at least a dozen reservations. But not Rich.

"You got it," he said after only a moment's hesitation. "Anything you want. I'll talk to the owner right away. We'll have the contract drawn up lickety-split. Promise. Just give me the details. What's the name of the bookstore and who's the owner?"

Alice hesitated. She knew what other question lay hidden within that one. *Where are you?* But she couldn't get Rich to help her without divulging where she'd run off to. To save her hideaway, she had to sacrifice her hiding place.

"Blithedale Books, it's called. In Blithedale."

She sighed. There. It was done.

CHAPTER 42

*D*espite being exhausted, Alice slept fitfully that night.

A single nightmare ran on repeat: She was back in the church, standing next to Rich at the altar. Except it was a massive cathedral. Like Notre Dame in Paris. And the walls were crumbling. The whole vaulted ceiling was going to collapse, yet no one was moving toward the exit. When she tried to run, Rich smiled and held her hand tight.

"Sweetheart," he said, his soft, lulling voice still loud and clear in the din of the collapsing cathedral. She looked down at their hands and he was putting her engagement ring back on her finger. "You lost this."

The ring was made of gold and shaped like a heart.

Alice woke with a gasp and sat up in bed. Her heart was galloping in her chest. She gripped the bedsheets.

On her bedside table lay her phone. No missed calls or messages. Of course not. Rich didn't need to call anymore. He was coming.

She ran a hand across her forehead, expecting to feel hot.

She did feel feverish. Clammy. Her mouth tasted like dust, and when she swallowed spit, her throat ached.

She put down the phone and noticed, curled up like a golden snake, the necklace she'd found in the bookstore. And next to it, the heart pendant. The wall and ceiling had collapsed because she'd wanted to get that damn pendant.

She picked up the necklace and pendant, and examined them closer.

Vince had bought multiple necklaces, each time adding a heart pendant. A necklace for each lover. And when he'd broken off the affair and paid attention to Susan again, he'd given his wife a heart pendant. Now she had three.

The fact that the pendant was a heart and not a dollar sign meant that Darrell Townsend wasn't the killer. If Darrell had been guilty of murder, he could have been removed as a threat to Blithedale Books. But it seemed Vince's death and Darrell's scheming had nothing to do with each other. Even if she exposed the killer, it wouldn't stop his development plans. Now she had to rely on Rich to save the bookstore.

The realization felt like a rock inside her chest, heavy and hard-edged.

Her phone buzzed. Rich again?

She reached for it. The message was from Becca. She'd sent a photo—a snapshot of a group of locals gathered in front of the What the Dickens Diner. Several held placards up with words written in marker pen:

Get well soon!
♥ *You've got friends*
Blithedale's thinking of you

Becca had obviously orchestrated this. Still, it didn't

diminish the message: People here cared enough to send her a message…

Her throat tightened, shutting the door on a sob. But she shook it off, refusing to let the emotion overcome her. And then she saw someone in the photo, and she sat up straight.

Andrea Connor, bald head and long, pendant earrings, stood at the edge of the crowd. She was back.

Alice reminded herself that catching the killer now wouldn't save the bookstore.

But if it hadn't been for Vince's death, this disaster wouldn't have happened. The Oriels would've bought the place. The bookstore would be safe.

She'd have to rely on Rich to save the bookstore. But she could rely on herself to solve the murder.

"You're the hero of your own story," her mom had once told her. "But a story is only a story if the hero takes action."

She swung her legs over the side of the bed.

Today would be her last day in Blithedale. Rich would take her home. But before she went back to her old life, she'd wrap up this case. She'd confront the killer.

CHAPTER 43

*A*lice sneaked out of the Pemberley Inn without being seen by Ona. She hurried along the sidewalk, head down, avoiding eye contact with any of the passersby.

She only looked up when she reached the bookstore. The back looked even more ruinous in the bright morning sunshine, and the gaping hole in the roof forced her to admit that the firefighters had been right to call the place unsafe.

Someone called her name from across the street. She pretended not to hear, turning away. She put her head down again and power-walked toward her destination.

Bonsai & Pie was open for business again. A customer tried to push open the door, her arms full of pie boxes. Alice held the door for her.

"Oh, thank you," the woman said, and then her eyes widened, apparently recognizing who she was speaking to. "Are you all right?"

The whole town must know what had happened. Heck, half of them had been standing in front of Blithedale Books when the wall collapsed. And, thanks to Becca, most of those people had gathered for a photo outside What the Dickens Diner.

Alice mumbled, "Fine, thanks," then slipped into the cafe.

Andrea stood behind the counter, serving another customer. She wore a tank top under an apron. Her neck, as before, was as bare as her head. It was like the gap in a puzzle, a piece conspicuously absent. This morning, Alice would complete the puzzle.

"Thank you," Andrea said. "And have a nice day."

The customer hurried out with his pie box, a hungry glint in his eyes.

Andrea turned her attention to Alice and put a hand to her chest.

"Alice," she said. "You had us all so worried. How are you feeling?"

She was a good actress. If Alice didn't know better, Andrea would've convinced her. But Alice's accident wouldn't make Vince's killer lose sleep. She knew Alice was asking questions. If the collapsing wall had killed Alice, wouldn't that have been convenient?

Once she'd assured Andrea that she was all right, she put her hand in her pocket and, watching Andrea, drew out the necklace with the heart pendant reattached.

"I believe this means a lot to you."

Andrea gasped and took a step back. Her face went rigid, yet her lips trembled when she said, "I don't know what you mean. Half of Blithedale owns a necklace."

"Vince bought this one."

"Vince," she said, and let out a long sigh. "How did you find it?"

Alice shook her head. "I found it at the bookstore."

Alice tried to speak as softly as she could, hoping Andrea had been bottling up this terrible secret and actually wanted to confess. "Vince had secrets. And he played with people's feelings. He played with your feelings, too, didn't he? Why don't you tell me what happened?"

Andrea put a hand to her cheek. Her eyes filled with tears.

"He said—" Her voice cracked. "He said he loved me. He bought me a necklace to prove we were one heart. He was making a lot of money and promised he'd take me places: France, Mexico, the Bahamas."

Her gaze became dreamy, sad, settling on something in the distance.

Alice said, "But he didn't take you, did he?"

Andrea shook her head. "He kept delaying. I'd ask when. He'd say soon. Finally, I confronted him. I said I couldn't keep this a secret any longer. I wanted us to be together. I wanted him to choose."

"You mean between you and Susan?"

Andrea nodded. "He said he'd leave her. Then delayed again. Until one night—" She stifled a sob. "He told me it was over. Just like that. Cold. Matter of fact. No more 'baby' or 'sweetheart.' He said, 'Andrea, you knew this couldn't last. Don't pretend—this isn't some girlie fantasy.' I couldn't believe how cruel he was. It was like I'd never known him." She gave a bitter laugh. "That was the real fantasy—the idea that he was a decent person. He was 100 percent selfish, only focused on himself and what he could get out of others."

"What happened then?"

Andrea shrugged. "Nothing. I went back to my old life. More alone than I'd ever felt. In fact, on the day he died, I closed the cafe for a while to visit MacDonald Realty. I'd been grappling with this idea—well, I might as well tell you. I decided to sell Bonsai & Pie."

"You what?" Alice had expected a denial of closing the store. "You went to Mayor MacDonald to talk about putting the cafe up for sale? On the day Vince died?"

"I did. But thank God nobody was there. They were out

of the office at meetings. So I took a long, long walk, all the way up into the woods. I have a little cabin. It's my hideaway."

The word sent a jolt through Alice.

Andrea said, "It's the only place I feel like myself. I can think things through. Does that make sense?"

Alice nodded.

"So that's what I did. I thought things through. My head cleared. Part of my heart did, too. I realized this: Vince was a jerk. He didn't deserve the grief I felt. By the time I returned to my cafe, I had dropped the idea of selling."

"After I talked to you, you went back, didn't you? You hid in the cabin."

"You could call it hiding," Andrea said. "I needed to think. Get clarity. If you knew about Vince, others would too. I'm not proud of having an affair with a married man. I thought I could keep it a secret. After giving it some thought, I decided I couldn't hide forever. I love this town. I love my little business."

"On the day Vince died, can anyone vouch for where you were?"

Andrea laughed. "Come on, Alice. You're joking. What is this—an interrogation?"

Something on Alice's face, maybe her seriousness, convinced Andrea that this was no joke.

"You think I killed Vince?"

"I found your necklace at the scene of the crime."

"But Alice," Andrea said, opening a drawer next to the display counter, "that's not my necklace."

She pulled out a necklace, identical to the one Alice was holding and held it up. It even had a single heart pendant.

"This is the necklace Vince gave me."

CHAPTER 44

*A*s Alice walked down Main Street, she felt confident she could rule out Andrea as a suspect. Andrea's revelation that she'd taken off Vince's necklace and put it in a drawer after their breakup convinced Alice that she hadn't killed him. Plus, her story about leaving town for her cabin—both on the day of Vince's death and when she fled from Alice's questions—made sense.

Back to square one...

And yet she was relieved that Andrea could be ruled out. Now the question was who the real killer might be. Vince's previous lovers—Sally and Harriet—no longer lived in Blithedale. Could one of them have returned? If they had, no one had seen them. And Becca was right—why return to kill Vince now?

But if the three hearts on Susan's pendant were all accounted for, who could the killer be? She recalled her conversation with Susan Malone, Vince's widow, and considered what she'd said about Vince's infidelities: "With each one, I'd allow myself to believe, you know, that maybe this time it would be different. It never was."

What if Vince had a new lover?

She reached the What the Dickens Diner. Before she delved deeper into who Vince's new lover might be, she had important business to see to. She needed to make sure Rich had kept his promise. She needed to make sure he saved what remained of her magical bookstore.

Inside the diner, Bunce sat in a booth with Mayor MacDonald and Chief Jimbo. But before Alice could reach them, Becca came rushing up to her. The big woman threw her arms around Alice in a bear hug, lifting her off the floor.

"I still can't believe you're all right."

"I was—" Alice let out an oof. "—until you crushed me."

Becca released her. "I have to tell you—you won't believe it—and you need to talk to Susan, she—"

"Wait," Alice said, holding up a hand to silence her. "First I have to speak to Bunce."

She ignored Becca's flurry of demands to talk and made a beeline for Bunce.

Striding over to where he sat, she interrupted the three men's conversation.

"Bunce, did you talk to Rich?"

"Why, hello, Alice," Mayor MacDonald said with a big smile.

Chief Jimbo gave a little wave.

Bunce squinted up at her, his usual frown on his face. "Mr. Rich?"

Her heart doubled over. Had Rich not called Bunce? "Rich Crawley?"

Bunce nodded. "Oh, yes. Mr. Crawley. I spoke with him."

"Well? What did you agree?"

"Nothing."

She stared at Bunce. "What do you mean *nothing*?"

"He made me an offer on the bookstore. But I said no."

"No?"

Alice grabbed Bunce by the shirt sleeve, balling the fabric into her fist.

"No?!"

"Got too much wax in your ears?" He shook himself free. "Did destroying my bookstore damage your ears? That's right. I said, *no*."

"But—but—why?"

"I may have an idea," Mayor MacDonald said. "When the Oriels backed out, it was because of Vince's death. Something about a ghost." He gave a little snort, showing his incredulity. "I remember sitting in this very booth with Bunce and Mr. and Mrs. Oriel, the four of us agreeing on the terms of the sale. It seemed a done deal. And at that very moment, Vince was falling to his death. Back then, the bookstore itself was still intact. But with half of it falling down, it now poses a risk to the community. I had no choice. I've officially required Bunce to fix the problem."

"But what am I, a millionaire?" Bunce snorted. "I don't have that kind of money. Mr. Crawley was unwilling to pay for fixing the bookstore building. He also balked at the idea of paying in cash. So I turned him down."

"But Bunce," Alice said, crouching down to get to his eye level, trying to be reasonable, "you're making impossible demands. Crazy demands. Who's going to pay in cash and invest in fixing the damage *before* they buy?"

Bunce crossed his arms. "Darrell Townsend will. In fact, he already has. I had no choice. We shook on it last night and signed this morning."

"Darrell's fixing the bookstore...?"

"Fixing?" Bunce grimaced. "Well, he's fixing it his way..."

CHAPTER 45

*T*here was a loud rumble from the street that Alice, in her shocked state, might have ignored—if she hadn't heard a kid call out from across the diner: "Look, Daddy, a bulldozer."

The kid was on his knees in a booth, hands planted on the window, staring out at Main Street. A massive bulldozer with its metal blade raised came trundling past the diner.

Everything was happening too fast. Like experiencing the wall and ceiling collapse all over again.

But this time Alice didn't stand frozen for long.

She bolted toward the diner's front door, ignoring Becca, who called her name.

Alice flung open the door and flew onto the sidewalk. She sprinted toward the bookstore, determined to catch the bulldozer and stop this madness.

But to her amazement, she wasn't the only one with this idea.

The bulldozer slowed and then came to a stop. A person blocked its path. It was Kris Cox, wearing her blazer and gold watch and brandishing a shovel.

"Go back," Kris yelled. "There'll be no destruction today."

Alice joined her. "Kris, what are you doing here?"

"I'm doing what I can to stop that bastard, Darrell Townsend, from destroying Blithedale. We can't let this happen. We can't let him hurt this town. It's precisely what he's planned all along."

The driver of the bulldozer, a man in a yellow hard hat, honked his horn. "Hey, get out of the way, ladies."

Alice ignored him. "But Darrell and Bunce signed—"

"The ink hasn't even dried," Kris said, cutting her off. "We can still get Darrell to back out. We've done it before. Are you with or against Darrell Townsend?"

"Uh," Alice said. "Against, of course."

"Good." Kris thrust the shovel at her. "You take this. Hold off the bulldozer. I'll go find Darrell—they say he's at home in that monstrosity in the woods—and I'll convince him to back out of the deal with Bunce."

"But how?"

"Let me worry about that," Kris said, already jogging away from the bookstore, heading down the street.

The bulldozer honked again, and the driver leaned out of his seat, glaring at Alice.

"I'm trying to do my job."

"But you can't just demolish the place. There are books inside. There's an old wardrobe with a red door that—"

Chief Jimbo shuffled toward them and said, "Everyone calm down."

He gave Alice's shovel a raised eyebrow and held out a hand.

"You're not going to hit anyone, are you?" There was a slight tremble to his voice and he kept his distance, even as he reached toward her. "You don't seem the type."

For once, Chief Jimbo was right. She wasn't the type. She

couldn't actually raise a weapon against this bulldozer driver, who was, as he'd said himself, only doing his job.

She lowered the shovel. "I can't—"

A pair of hands wrapped around her from behind. Chief Jimbo leapt forward and yanked the shovel from her hands.

"Hey," she cried out, glancing back at the man who'd grabbed her. "Let me go."

Another man in a hard hat. He was dragging her away, her heels scraping against the blacktop. She struggled to free herself, but he'd managed to lock her in a tight embrace.

"Calm down, lady," the guy said. "Just calm down."

She would've liked to kick him. But a roar went up from the bulldozer and it lurched forward, and instead of kicking, she screamed, "No, stop!"

But the bulldozer didn't stop. It barrelled forward, straight into the front of the bookstore building. There was a sickening crunch as it tore into the brick, punching a giant hole. Then it backed away, and Alice wiggled free from the man's grip and jumped forward. But Chief Jimbo stood in her way, hands held up.

"It's not safe, Miss Hartford. Not safe."

Before she could get around him, the bulldozer had crashed into the bookstore again, this time setting off a chain reaction. Much of the rest of the wall fell. Then the ceiling, no longer having enough support, either on the front or the back, collapsed.

An enormous crash. Dust rising in a great cloud.

The whole bookstore lay in ruin.

And then her tears came. They ran down her face and she stumbled backward into someone's embrace. She didn't bother to look who it was. She couldn't tear her gaze free from the disaster in front of her.

As she watched the bulldozer drive into Blithedale Books again, felling the remaining wall, sobs shook her body. The bookstore—her beloved bookstore—it was a ruin, the wardrobe crushed, her red door gone. The memories of her childhood and her mom, all the best parts of her life, had collapsed into a heap of rubble.

The hands that held her tightened. A man's hands. She turned, her eyes blurred with tears, and saw him.

"It's all right. I'm here now."

Rich wrapped his arms around her, gathering her into a straightjacket hug.

CHAPTER 46

"*A*re you comfortable?"

Rich took off his cardigan. He balled it up and stuffed it down behind Alice's back, providing her with extra cushioning against the leatherette seat in the diner booth.

"Do you need another drink? How about something to eat? A muffin? Did you even have a proper, balanced breakfast? Low blood sugar is no joke."

He looked around and waved and called out, "Excuse me, would you mind bringing a menu? We'd like something to eat."

Turning back to Alice, he added, "Maybe a cup of soothing, herbal tea would be a good idea. Calm the nerves, you know? You're very upset about this bookstore business."

Alice stared at the formica table, its gray base dotted with a million black spots, like white noise on an old disconnected TV. That's how she felt. Broken. Her mind a swirl of fragments, shards of thoughts, voices drowned out by a steady roar.

Sure, she heard Rich's droning voice, but the ceaseless sympathy and eager questioning meant little.

She'd watched the workers demolish her beloved bookstore. Blithedale Books was gone, smashed to dust, the wardrobe with the red door a pile of splinters, her hideaway a mere memory.

What did she have left, except her old life with Rich?

"Here you go," a familiar voice said. Becca. Out of the corner of her eye, Alice noticed menus being placed on the table. "Let me know when you're ready to order."

She left them, a soft sneaker footfall moving away. This was how it would be. Now that Rich had returned—now that he'd taken her back—Becca would keep her distance, no longer offering gossip or sympathy. Ona, too.

And it didn't matter since, in an hour or two, Alice would be sitting in Rich's car, starting the long drive back to the city.

Except it did matter.

Alice wished it was Becca and Ona sitting next to her in the booth, not Rich. She had come to Blithedale to make sure her mom's bookstore lived on, but something surprising had happened along the way: She'd made friends. She'd rediscovered what a wonderful place this town was—this home she had shared with her mom.

She wished she could make sense of her feelings. She wished she could fight what felt inevitable. But her strength had left her. The destruction of the bookstore had drained her almost completely. Then Rich had finished her off, delivering the death blow. A soft, gentle death blow.

She was done. She would go back with Rich and he'd sweeten her up until she was ready to walk down the aisle again.

The helter-skelter black dots in the formica table danced in front of her eyes. Then tears trickled down her cheeks.

"Oh, sweetheart," Rich said. He reached across her to grab napkins from the dispenser, balling them up and dabbing gently at her face. "Your heart is broken. But even a broken heart can be mended. We'll take a vacation, you and me. After all, we do still have the reservations for our honeymoon. Still want to go to Hay-on-Wye? What am I saying? Of course, you do. Even if you don't feel like it now, you'll feel better once we're in the bookshop capitol of the world."

He prattled on about Hay-on-Wye and the beautiful Welsh countryside, and Alice stared at the formica pattern, seeing nothing but the chaos of white noise.

"Alice," Becca said from far, far away. Alice willed herself —it took a great effort—to turn her head and look up. Becca, head cocked in a show of concern, said, "You have a phone call up at the counter."

Alice shook her head, unable to say the words, "No, I can't do it right now."

"Sure you can," Becca said, as if she'd heard her thoughts. "Mr. Crawley, she needs your help."

It was the right thing to say to Rich, of course. He sprang into action, slipping a hand under her arm and guiding her out of the booth. "There, there, sweetheart. You can do it. It's just a phone call."

Once Alice was on her feet, Becca stepped in, like she was stealing Rich's dance partner, nudging him away. "I'll take it from here, Mr. Crawley. Sit down and I'll bring coffee for both of you."

"Oh, don't you think, though—?"

"She'll need you right here when she comes back."

"Right." Rich reluctantly sat down. "I'll be right here."

Alice allowed Becca to lead her to the counter.

"Here you go, Alice." Becca grabbed an old phone with a coiled wire and handed it to Alice. "You'll want to hear what this is about. Meanwhile, I'll keep Rich company."

Becca winked at her, then moved over to Rich. What was going on?

Alice put the receiver to her ear. "Hello?"

"Is Rich looking?" Ona said. "Can he see you?"

Something about the urgency in her voice cleared part of the white noise from Alice's mind.

She looked over. Becca had blocked Rich's view. In fact, she bent over him, pointing at the menu and describing the merits of every item, one at a time.

"No," Alice said.

"Good," Ona said. "Because we're getting you out of there."

CHAPTER 47

$\mathcal{B}$ehind the diner, Ona's pickup truck stood parked by the trash cans. Ona herself leaned against the driver's door, a toothpick in her mouth.

"You coming or staying?" she asked.

"Where are we going?"

"To finish what you started."

Alice rubbed her eyes. It seemed the sun was brighter, the haze of white noise clearing, and every detail crisper—from the wide tires on the pickup to the sparkling rhinestones on Ona's eyepatch.

She looked back over her shoulder. The back door to the diner had shut behind her. Beyond it, Rich was waiting for her. Beyond it lay her old life.

She took a deep breath and let it out. She'd run from Rich once. She'd do it again. Except this time, she knew what she was running toward. Toward Ona and Becca—and Blithedale.

Slipping onto the passenger seat of the pickup, she said, "It's like you're breaking me out of prison."

"Not a bad metaphor." Ona reached across and grabbed

173

Alice's hand and gave it a warm squeeze. "That's what friends are for."

Alice put her hand over Ona's and held it there for a moment. Ona and Becca cared so much for her—worried so much about her going back to Rich—that they'd conspired to save her. The realization sent waves of warmth through her body, and exhausted as she was, the feeling of being loved brought tears to her eyes.

Ona said, "Let's get going."

She put the car in reverse and revved the engine. As they swung out onto Main Street, Alice, gripping the truck's grab handle, asked, "But really, where are we going?"

"Susan Malone's. After the bookstore collapsed, she talked to Becca. Said that when she heard the news, she was worried for a moment that you'd died. She regretted not being honest with you when you visited. She wanted another chance."

"I'm all about second chances," Alice said, realizing now why Becca had been so excited when she'd first come into the diner. "But what couldn't Susan tell me the first time?"

"We'll find out."

They'd already crossed town, and the pickup turned onto the street with the modest ranch houses. A minute later, Alice spotted the Malones' home, with Vince's sports car in the driveway.

Ona parked the pickup. As soon as Alice got out, the front door to the house opened and Susan appeared. She hugged herself, staring at Alice and Ona with obvious nervousness.

She looked up and down the street. "Come inside."

Alice and Ona followed Susan inside the house. This time, Susan didn't offer coffee on the porch. She brought them to the kitchen and stopped. She went to the espresso machine, then turned back. Went to the electric kettle, then turned away. She couldn't seem to decide where to go or what to do.

"How do I do this?" she asked no one in particular.

"You start," Alice said, putting a comforting hand on Susan's arm, "at the beginning."

Susan reached for a pack of cigarettes on the kitchen island and held it in her hands. But she didn't pull out a cigarette and light it.

"Years ago, Vince started making more money than he'd ever made before. When did it begin?" She sighed. "It began with that cabin—the Oriels' summer house—which fell into the gorge."

CHAPTER 48

"**I** knew something was fishy," Susan said. "Vince played fast and loose with the facts. He loved to tell tall tales. Hell, he played fast and loose with his marriage. But he was good at his job. So how could he have messed up the Oriels' cabin so badly that half of it collapsed into the gorge?"

She shook her head, her gaze turning inward.

"Did you confront him?" Alice asked.

"Not at first. Not even when he came home with more cash than I'd ever seen. 'So, wait a minute, Vince. You screw up more than you've ever screwed up in your life, and your pockets are full of dough. What's going on?' That's what I should've said, only I didn't. Maybe I was glad to have the money. Maybe it was nice to pay the bills and still have enough money for a new TV, too."

"But it wasn't just a new TV."

"No, it wasn't. There were more jobs. He got more subtle, you know. Accidents would happen, but people no longer connected the accidents with the contracting work."

Alice looked to Ona, and Ona mouthed the word, "Wow."

But neither interrupted Susan, who went on: "I never knew if a job was legit or one of his sabotage jobs. Until after. Sometimes long after, when a building would fail an inspection. But as soon as he started on Blithedale Books, I had a bad feeling. Then—"

She gave in and pulled a cigarette out of the pack and lit it. She shoved the lighter and cigarette pack away from on the countertop, as if they disgusted her. Still, she inhaled.

She exhaled a cloud of smoke and said, "Then, a couple of weeks ago, I overhear him talking on the phone. Sweet talk, you know? Obviously, he's talking to whoever his new lover is, and he's bragging about how this big client is paying him to fix the bookstore so it'll fall apart. Then backtracking, as if the story's upset his lover—got her mad. 'Aw, sweetheart,' he's telling her, 'don't worry—I wouldn't do anything to hurt this town.'" Susan snorted, shaking her head in disbelief. "I wonder if she believed that load of bull."

Alice's heart thumped in her chest. This was incredible. The truth was coming out. "Did he mention the client's name? Or the lover's name? It wasn't Andrea, was it?"

"Not Andrea, no. He dumped her the last time I threatened to leave him." She fingered her necklace with the heart pendants. "I don't know who his new lover was. But I did hear who was paying him to sabotage the bookstore. It's not hard to guess."

"Darrell Townsend," Alice said.

Susan smiled a crooked smile. "Bingo."

CHAPTER 49

*A*lice slapped a hand on the pickup's dashboard.

"I knew it," she said. "Darrell's been crooked this whole time. But I got the crime wrong. He didn't kill Vince. He paid Vince to sabotage the bookstore."

"And the cabin. Poor Mr. and Mrs. Oriel."

Ona pulled out of Susan Malone's driveway, and they drove down the street, ranch houses flitting past the window.

Ona said, "So Darrell paid Vince to sabotage the bookstore, expecting the wall and ceiling to collapse later."

"Which it did," Alice said, "and almost killed me."

"Then Darrell would swoop in and offer Bunce a cheap price for the property, plus cleanup. Like he's done now. All along, it's been about his business and his plan for Blithedale. But there's something I don't understand. Why sabotage the Oriels' summer house deep in the woods?"

"That was personal," Alice said. "Think about it. Who bought the property?"

"Of course. Darrell did. And he built his own house on the Oriels' old property."

"Right. He probably saw the property and thought it was the perfect location for his dream home."

"Dream home?" Ona grimaced. "That ugly box he built?"

Alice looked out the window at houses and trees flashing past.

"That may have been the first time Darrell paid Vince to do sabotage. He started with something he wanted for himself, then realized, after he'd gotten the land from the Oriels, that he could apply the same technique to other properties around Blithedale."

"And us protesters wouldn't get in his way," Ona said, "because the authorities would back him up—independent inspections would show that a building had become dangerous."

The mention of protesters sparked something at the back of Alice's mind. She thought of the photo in Bonsai & Pie of Andrea and others blocking one of Darrell's development projects.

"I thought Andrea killed Vince, because he broke off their relationship. But Andrea didn't drop her necklace."

"The new lover did," Ona said.

Alice nodded. "It was a new relationship. Susan had just discovered it, and hadn't threatened Vince again. As far as we know, the lover had no reason to feel spurned. So she didn't kill Vince because he'd broken her heart."

"Then why did she kill Vince? And who is she?"

"Remember what Susan said she heard Vince say on the phone? He bragged about sabotaging the bookstore and the lover got upset. *Aw, sweetheart,* he said, *don't worry—I wouldn't do anything to hurt this town.*"

"Wait, you're telling me Vince's lover killed him to stop the sabotage?"

"That's right." Alice could feel all the pieces of puzzle slot into place. "Here's what I think happened: She goes to confront him at the bookstore. Maybe she plans to murder him. Or maybe Vince refuses to stop the sabotage, and she gets mad, shoving him off the scaffolding. Either way, her love for Blithedale is much bigger than her love for Vince ever was."

She looked over at Ona as they rolled down Main Street. A chill went down her spine. Goosebumps prickled her arms. She knew who the killer was.

"Turn around, Ona. We have to get to Darrell Townsend's home in the woods and fast."

Alice remembered then what the killer wore: a gold watch. She'd been wearing a matching gold necklace the first time she saw her. But not afterward. She'd said, "I'm doing what I can to stop that bastard, Darrell Townsend, from destroying Blithedale."

"To Darrell's?" Ona asked. "Why?"

"Because if we don't get there quick, Kris Cox is going to kill him."

CHAPTER 50

*O*na took a different road into the woods than the one the Oriels had taken. This one led to Darrell's main entrance, a paved road stretching through the forest to a bridge over the gorge.

Alice leaned forward and looked out the windshield. Up ahead lay Darrell's box of a house. They'd approached the front. The deck overlooking the gorge was on the other side.

Ona slammed on the brakes. Alice's seatbelt dug into her shoulder. The pickup screeched to a halt.

"Look," Ona said. "Kris's car."

A car stood parked on the narrow bridge across the gorge, blocking access.

"We'll have to walk the rest of the way."

"Let's call the cops," Alice said. "But not Chief Jimbo. The state police."

"Good idea." Ona brought out her phone. She looked up at Alice. "No reception."

Alice cursed. Checking her phone, she saw the same. "Me neither. Listen, Ona, we don't know what Kris has planned.

It may be dangerous. You drive back to the main road and call the cops when you've got enough bars on your phone again."

"If it's dangerous, I'm coming with you."

"We need to get to Darrell as quickly as possible. But we also need to call the cops. And I don't drive stick."

Ona stared at her, a defiant glint in her eye.

"Please, Ona. We don't have time."

"Fine," Ona said. "Go."

Alice opened the door and slipped down from the seat. She heard the pickup's engine rumble to life, but didn't bother to look back.

Reaching Kris's car, she put a foot on the fender and climbed up on the back. She scrambled over the roof and slid down the windshield onto the hood. Then she was on the other side and ran up the drive toward the house.

The drive curved upward, leading to the front door. As she jogged toward the house, she hoped Kris didn't know she was coming. Had she heard the pickup?

Above her head, the windows were matte black squares, blackout shades obscuring the interior. But since she couldn't look in, it also meant no one could see her approach.

At the front door, she hesitated. Then put her hand on the handle and pushed down. Without even a click, the door slid open. It swung inward, soft and silent.

Inside, she found herself in a high-ceilinged hallway. Stairs to the right led upward. A passage to the left opened onto a living room. A corridor straight ahead gave her a glimpse of a kitchen and wide windows.

Considering the layout from the outside, the deck must be somewhere straight ahead.

She stepped into the living room, peeking around the corner first to make sure no one was there. A big sofa set with two arm chairs, everything in black leather. A widescreen TV on the wall, also black. A black glass coffee table. Bookshelves done in a black finish. Only the floor provided a contrast: hardwood floors with a white rug.

Another doorway to her right. She peeked around the corner.

The kitchen. A cup of coffee lay on the black marble counter, overturned, brown liquid dripping onto the white-tiled floor and forming a puddle.

She crept forward. The back wall consisted of glass, black shades pulled down to keep out the sun. But a sliding door stood open, and as Alice crept toward it, she heard voices.

"This is insane," Darrell was saying.

There was a grating sound, like a saw biting into wood. She moved to the sliding door, making sure to position her body behind the blackout shades.

Peering through the open door, she saw Darrell.

Her heart did a somersault.

Darrell sat in a chair, heavy duct tape wound around his chest and arms and legs. Beyond him, Kris crouched down by the guardrail, sawing into the posts. She'd already cut into several of them.

Kris stopped sawing. She cocked her head and gave the post a hefty whack with her hand. It splintered.

"Nice sabotage, wouldn't you agree, Darrell? Vince would be proud of me."

"You're insane," Darrell said. "No one will believe it was an accident. How does a man who's tied up to a chair fall into a gorge accidentally? They'll know I was murdered."

Kris laughed. "Oh, don't worry. I'll clean things up, so your death doesn't look suspicious. After all, no one suspected Vince's death was anything but an accident, least of all Chief Jimbo."

"I suspected," Alice said, stepping through the door.

Kris stood up. For a moment, she gaped. But then recovered before Alice could do anything. Kris leaped toward Darrell, grabbed the back of the chair, and hauled him across the deck, the chair legs grating on the wood.

"Wait," Alice said. "Don't do this, Kris."

The knuckles on Kris's hands were white. Her face was wild with desperation, eyes wide, jaw muscles tense. "I'll throw him over the edge. I'll do it."

"And then what? Are you going to throw me over, too?"

Alice took a step closer. Kris frowned, clearly thinking about that, looking down at Darrell and back up at Alice.

"I wanted to save the bookstore, too," Alice said.

"Then you understand why I have to do this. Darrell won't stop, unless we stop him. Once he's gone, Blithedale can grow in a healthy way. I love this town. I've never lived in a place that's felt like home. Blithedale was meant to be full of books and arts and culture—that was Old Mayor Townsend's vision. He had a plan."

She let go with one hand and reached behind her.

Alice's heart leapt into her throat. Did Kris have a gun? Was she going to pull out a knife? But Kris whipped out a little leather-bound book, small enough to fit in a pocket.

"This was his journal," Kris said. "He jotted down every idea he had for the town, and it's like an entire blueprint for a happy, thriving community."

"You stole it," Darrell said.

"I saved it. I took it before you could destroy it."

Darrell snorted. "Destroy it? Why would I do that? It's just an old book. Besides, I've never had any interest in my grandfather's vision for Blithedale. That was a long time ago. He was a kook. I've got my own, modern vision for what this town will become."

"It's a vision of hell," Kris spluttered, her face contorting with anger, and she pulled Darrell closer to the broken guardrail.

"You're right," Alice said, reaching a hand toward Kris. She needed to keep the conversation going. She needed to keep Kris from throwing Darrell into the gorge. "You're right, Kris. Darrell's vision for Blithedale is terrifying. And he's willing to achieve it by lying and sabotaging. Which you discovered, didn't you?"

Kris nodded. "Vince bragged about it. All the money he was getting from Darrell. But when I got upset, he dismissed my worries. He wouldn't stop. Bunce and I planned to meet with the Oriels to finalize the sale of the bookstore, but Mayor MacDonald offered to take over. He often likes to step in and close a deal. I could have insisted. It was my deal, after all. But I didn't. I saw my chance to head back to the bookstore and confront Vince while he was alone."

Alice remembered a detail she'd glossed over—when she'd found Bunce with Mayor MacDonald and Chief Jimbo at the diner, the mayor had given her the clue to Kris's absence. He'd said, "I remember sitting in this very booth with Bunce and Mr. and Mrs. Oriel, the four of us agreeing on the terms of the sale." They hadn't been five people, as they would've been if Kris had stayed.

"But Vince was cocky," Kris continued. "When I confronted him on the scaffolding, he refused to stop his work. He told me to go to hell. I gave him a shove. We wrestled, he tripped over his toolbox and lost his balance, and I barrelled into him, driving him over the edge. He tried to grab me as he fell. He caught hold of my necklace and tore it off."

"You left it behind," Alice said.

"I couldn't find it. I heard a sound, and I panicked and ran."

"When you learned what Vince was doing, why didn't you report it?"

"To Chief Jimbo? Or Mayor MacDonald? No one would've believed me."

Darrell struggled against his bonds. "And no one will now. Will they believe a crazy killer? Or a hysterical runaway bride? Unlikely."

Alice heard a sound behind her and turned. Ona stepped through the sliding door. She was holding up her phone.

"They might not believe Kris or Alice," she said, "but they'll believe my video recording. Oh, and what's that sweet music I hear drifting through the woods?"

Sirens wailed far away, coming closer and closer.

"The police," Ona said.

"But how did you manage to call the cops and get here so fast?" Alice asked.

Ona grinned. "I figured Darrell must have a landline since he lived in a house that got no cell phone reception. I was right. So I followed you into the house, called the police, and then started recording these confessions. It was a risk, but I wasn't going to leave you alone with a killer and a crook."

"I'm not a crook," Darrell said, his face turning red. He fought against his bonds. His eyes darted this way and that, desperate, like a trapped animal. But the duct tape was too tight.

There was a loud crash. Kris had thrown herself at the guardrail, smashing the weakened struts.

Alice dove toward her.

Kris flew through the broken railing just as Alice tackled her, hooking her right arm around the woman's midriff.

But gravity was already pulling Kris down over the edge of the deck, and Alice felt the weight drag her along.

She threw out her left arm and caught one of the guardrail struts. It stopped her—and her other arm tugged

Kris back. Then there was a sickening rip as the sabotaged wood splintered and broke apart, and her arm came free.

She slid forward.

She screamed.

Gravity yanked her over the side.

CHAPTER 51

"*G*otcha!" Ona yelled.

Alice dangled over the gorge, head down, as hands clamped onto her ankles. Her own right arm still hooked Kris's midriff, but she was slipping. Alice brought her left arm around, too, praying Kris wouldn't wriggle in her grip. She'd be sure to drop her, then. But Kris didn't move. She hung limply in Alice's grip, pure dead-weight, trembling.

"I can't pull you up," Ona said. "I don't know how much longer I can hold on…"

Alice looked down. Darrell's deck jutted out over the gorge. If they fell, she and Kris would plummet down, down, down. A stream gurgled and splashed among the rocks, but it would be no safety net—they'd drop straight onto giant boulders.

Kris slipped in her grip. Her shirt was riding up. Alice tried to tighten her hold, but the woman was sliding out of her embrace.

Voices came from above. Someone called out, "Police!"

Footsteps. Then more voices. And Ona crying out, "Over here—help us!"

Alice gritted her teeth. *Please, please, come quick.*

Kris was sliding away from her. Even if help came quick, Alice would drop her.

"Kris, listen to me," Alice said. "I need you to reach up and put your hands around me. Grab me. Like you're hugging me. Can you do that?"

Kris turned her head and met Alice's eyes. Kris looked dazed, as if she'd woken from a deep sleep. She must be in shock.

Alice repeated her instructions. "Can you do that?"

Kris nodded. She reached out, her arms moving slowly, as if in a dream, and finally reaching around Alice's body. Alice felt Kris's fingers dig into her back as she held on.

"Good," Alice said. "Hold on tight. I've got you. We're doing this together. I'm not letting you go and you're not letting me—"

Ona's grip on Alice's ankles slipped and Alice jolted downward.

Kris screamed and she gripped Alice with surprising strength, squeezing the air out of Alice's lungs. They were meshed together tightly now. If one fell, the other would fall too. But at least Alice wouldn't have to live with the guilt of letting Kris drop into the gorge...

Then hands gripped her calves and pulled her upward. Then more hands seized her thighs and she heard someone say, "Steady, steady," and her legs scraped against the wood of the deck—her knees bumped against it—as the view of the gorge below swung away as she was hauled up.

A dozen hands dragged them both onto the deck.

She held on to Kris. They clung together, and Kris curled up in a ball and sobbed. Alice stroked her back.

"It's all right. It's all over now."

CHAPTER 52

*A*lice stared at the empty lot where the bookstore had once been.

It had been a week since she'd solved the case. Kris, having confessed, was in jail for the murder of Vince Malone. Darrell had been arrested for his role in sabotaging the bookstore, and he was under investigation for at least half a dozen other such criminal acts, including conspiring to destroy the Oriels' cabin. Townsend Development had been shuttered. His brother Todd had skipped town.

Everything was wrapped up.

Or almost everything.

Whenever she walked past the empty lot where the bookstore had been, her heart seized up, as if a hand were squeezing it. And this morning, she'd felt a punch to her gut too, as she'd spotted a sign on a stake driven into the ground. It was from MacDonald Realty and said, "SOLD."

As she gazed at the sign, footsteps approached.

"We thought we might find you here," Ona said.

She and Becca stood on either side of Alice, joining her in

looking at the empty lot and the sign. Becca handed Alice a take-out cup of coffee.

"Thanks," Alice said, and sipped her coffee.

They all drank their coffees in silence.

"So…?" Ona said.

"So what?" Alice asked.

"Please," Becca said. "The anticipation is killing us. You met Rich last night. Well, what happened?"

Alice smiled. She could count on her friends wanting to know every detail of her life. It was nice to know they cared.

"After Kris and Darrell were arrested, I told him I needed time and space…"

"We know that," Ona said. "Skip ahead. What happened last night?"

"Well, I told the truth. I said I couldn't come back to my old life. I'd never be happy with him, no matter how hard he tried. Then I gave him back the engagement ring and wished him all the best."

Ona put a hand on Alice's back. "I'm proud of you. That must've been hard."

"Yeah, it was hard. But it would've been harder if I'd stayed with him."

In fact, Rich had cried and begged and even bribed her with a bookstore of her own and an annual "alone vacation." But she hadn't wavered. She hoped he would find a partner who would thrive in the bubble of attentiveness he loved to create. In fact, she was sure he would eventually find the right person. It just wasn't her.

"So, now what?" Ona asked.

Alice shrugged. "Now I take some time to figure out what I do next. Who knows, maybe whoever bought the property from Bunce will build a new bookstore and I can get a job as the manager. After all, it turns out that Old Mayor Townsend always intended for there to be a bookstore in this location."

She pulled out the old notebook from her back pocket. Ona and Becca leaned in to take a closer look.

"See, this is a map of Blithedale," Alice explained. "And the old mayor sketched the businesses he envisioned coming in. You can see the diner. He calls it a restaurant. Of course, the Pemberley Inn is labeled as 'mayor's residence.'"

"The old fox wouldn't give up his own house, huh?" Ona said.

"Actually, later in the notebook, he notes that when he dies, he'd like the house to be turned into an inn." Alice closed the book and tapped the front. "It's amazing. You can see today's Blithedale in these pages—much of his vision was on the way to becoming a reality."

"Until his grandson, Darrell, got in the way," Becca said. "Well, now's our chance to continue the good work Old Mayor Townsend started so many years ago."

Alice sighed. "That's assuming the people who bought from Bunce are interested in establishing a bookstore here."

"Well, that's up to you," Ona said.

"Me? How do you figure that?"

Ona smiled and looked at Becca, who gave a little nod, then said, "Ona and I took the liberty of pooling some of our savings. Plus, we ran a little fundraiser. All very hush-hush. Together, we managed to raise enough funds that we had enough to buy the lot from Bunce."

"What?" Alice gaped at Becca, then at Ona. "When were you going to tell me?"

"Now," Ona said. "We wanted you to talk to Rich first. We didn't want to sway your decision."

"But we hoped…" Becca added.

"Oh, yes," Ona grinned. "We hoped."

"So, you mean…" Alice was trying to make sense of it. "The two of you bought the property?"

Becca said, "Actually, the newly established 'Blithedale

Future Fund' bought it. For too long, we've let the likes of Darrell Townsend shape this town. Now we, the people who love Blithedale, will invest in its future, and we want you to be the first recipient."

Alice was at a loss for words.

I don't know what to say."

"Just say 'yes, please,'" Ona said, laughing.

Alice had come to town to preserve the bookstore and the memories that continued to live within it. She'd failed. But instead she'd discovered that Blithedale could contain new experiences—she could make new happy memories worthy of the ones she'd made with her mom. And now Becca and Ona were giving her a chance to build on her old memories in the very place where her mom's bookstore had stood. Yes, Blithedale Books was gone forever. But now it could be reborn.

Despite the excitement, despite her profound gratitude for what her friends were willing to do for her—not just her friends, but everyone in Blithedale who'd donated to the new fund—she told herself this was too big a gift. She couldn't rely on their charity.

"You're giving me the property? I can't accept that."

Becca held up a hand. "Not giving, no. We set the fund up so that we could help you, but we want to help others, too. The Blithedale Future Fund gives loans or makes investments. The fund has bought the property, the way the bank might give you a mortgage."

"Except our mortgage interest rates are much better," Ona said with a wink. "The property's yours if you want it."

Alice's said, "I'll pay you back."

"That's right," Becca said. "That's the deal."

Alice let out a laugh. A loan was different. She could accept a loan. Even if it was the most generous thing she'd ever experienced.

"You two are amazing, you know that?"

She threw her arms around Ona and then Becca, nearly dousing both of them with coffee.

Then she stepped back and surveyed the property. Then thought: *Loans have to be repaid. And how am I supposed to make enough money to repay a loan when I don't have enough to rebuild?*

The weight of reality settled on her shoulders, deflating her.

"But I still can't accept this offer. It takes money to build a whole new bookstore, let alone stock it."

"Don't you have savings?" Becca asked.

"That would be enough for the books and getting started. But constructing a building? No way."

"Lucky you," Ona said, grinning, "I have one to spare."

CHAPTER 53

*P*aper lanterns bobbed on wires overhead, casting soft, colorful light. The local bluegrass band played gentle, folksy jazz. A crowd of people thronged Thor's cocktail stand on the sidewalk, laughing and talking.

At another stand, Andrea was serving pie to just as great success.

But the biggest throng of people milled around the entrance to the tiny house at the center of what used to be an empty lot. The tiny house—a log cabin crammed full of books—had an important detail: a red door.

As Alice approached the scene with another box of books in her arms, she couldn't help but smile. She still couldn't believe it. It had taken only a month and here it was—her own bookstore. Ona had designed and built the tiny house, using remnants of the old Blithedale Books, including bits of wood from the red wardrobe. Alice loved the symbolism of it: The bookstore had been reborn.

The sign above the door said:

WONDERLAND BOOKS

195

Finally, a hideaway she could fit into. A Wonderland made just for her. It was perfect. As her mom had once told her, "A house is made of four walls; a home is made of love." Alice loved Wonderland Books, and in a way she couldn't explain, she knew her mom did too.

"Excuse me," she said. "Coming through."

Inside the tiny store, people stood by the built-in bookshelves or sat perched on the benches against the wall, sampling novels or memoirs or histories of this-that-and-the-other. Alice plonked down the box on the little counter.

"Just in the nick of time," Ona said from behind the counter. She wore one of her Regency dresses. "Do you have a copy of *The Shadow of the Wind*?"

Alice dug into the box and found the novel by Carlos Ruiz Zafón, a magical tale about books and mysteries, one she often recommended to friends. Now she would recommend it to her customers.

Ona rang up the sale. Becca moved around the little space with a tray of canapés, her own contribution to the grand opening party. She bent down to offer one to Mayor MacDonald, who was sitting on a bench in his white suit, engrossed in a copy of *Life on the Mississippi* by Mark Twain. Esther Lucas, the consignment store owner, came to the counter with a stack of books.

"I love reading," she told Alice. "But honestly, I never enjoyed going into Bunce's bookstore. I ordered my books online. I'm so happy I can come here instead and support your store."

Alice glanced at the stack of books, and was surprised by the range of authors Esther had picked out: Robin Hobb, Alexander McCall Smith, Margery Allingham, Anthony Trollope, and Richard Osman.

"You read widely."

"To me, it's like travel. The whole point is to go far from where you began."

Alice nodded, appreciating the wisdom of those words. She herself had come far, even if she'd come right back to where she began—a bookstore in Blithedale.

After unboxing the books, Alice took over from Ona, ringing up more and more sales. She knew she wouldn't have as many customers on an ordinary day, but she also knew that this was a good sign for her little bookstore's success.

And her new life in Blithedale.

Ona and Becca joined her at the counter, Becca putting down the empty canapé tray.

Alice took Ona's hand, then Becca's hand. "You know what I realized again tonight?"

"Oh, no—another revelation about the murder?" Ona said.

"Something Darrell did that we didn't realize?" Becca asked.

Alice laughed and shook her head.

"I realized tonight that when I ran out on my wedding, I thought I was running away from love, when, in fact, I was throwing myself right into it."

She pulled her two friends into a warm hug. She'd never felt happier in her entire life. Who needed a hideaway when you had a home?

T hank you so much for visiting Blithedale. Join Alice and her friends for another cozy mystery in book 2:

A Theater to Die For

Oh, and want a FREE short story? Sign up for my newsletter updates on new books and I'll send the free story to you by email:

https://mpblackbooks.com/newsletter/

Finally, if you enjoyed this book, please take a moment to leave a review online. It makes it easier for other readers to find the book. Thanks so much!

Turn the page to read chapter 1 of *A Theater to Die For* (Book 2)...

A THEATER TO DIE FOR EXCERPT

"*D*id you see this?" Ona Rodriguez slapped a folded newspaper down on the bookstore counter. She unfolded the paper and read the headline of an article aloud, "Death Trap Bookstore Transforms into Wonderland."

"Is it—?"

Alice Hartford reached out and snatched the paper from Ona, making her friend laugh. Ona wore an eye-patch with red rhinestones that glittered in the light from the bookstore lamps. It somehow made her look even more excited.

Alice scanned the article. It was down at the bottom of the page, tucked into the corner, and only two paragraphs long. But it didn't matter. A major city newspaper had written a favorable review of her little bookstore.

She read the review and then read it again. It mentioned her as, "The runaway bride who endeared herself to the community by solving a local murder case." More importantly, the journalist called the bookstore, "An oasis for book lovers, and despite its tiny setting—or because of it—well worth a visit to this off-the-beaten-track town."

"Imagine if we can get more reviews like this," Alice said. "Imagine what it will do for Blithedale."

Ona grinned, apparently as excited about it as Alice.

"Just wait till we open for the Blithedale Future Fund applications," Ona said.

Alice said nothing. She looked away, hoping she wouldn't blush. The three friends—Alice, Ona, and Becca— were meeting this Sunday afternoon to discuss the Blithedale Future Fund and the upcoming applications for new loans.

Alice had been keeping a big secret from Ona and Becca, and in the days ahead of their meeting, she'd been so sure they would approve of the work she'd done. Now she was beginning to doubt herself.

"I know what you're thinking," Ona said.

Alice's gut tightened. "You do?"

"Sure. You're thinking the process I designed for applications is overly formal—that it's bureaucratic. But it'll make it'll easier in the long run."

"Was it hard when you chose to support my bookstore?"

"Oh, no. It was easy." Ona smiled. "Easiest decision I ever made. But this is different. We're opening up to anyone with an idea. We'll be flooded with applicants. And we want it to be open and inclusive, don't you agree?"

Alice nodded, her lips pressed together.

Ona said, "Once we've helped more local businesses, the newspapers will be buzzing. And, for once, the stories won't be about murder. They'll be about the Blithedale Future Fund. Speaking of the fund, where's Becca?"

Ona dug into a pocket and brought out an old-fashioned pocket watch, opening it and checking the time.

"It's past 5 pm. She'd better hurry."

She shut the watch with a snap and slipped it into her pocket again.

"We've got a lot to talk about if we're going to open for applications next week."

Trying to hide her emotions, Alice dug into her box of book donations, which she'd been sorting when Ona walked in.

Alice had held off telling them about Dorothy Bowers and the Blithedale Theater—and how she'd encouraged Dorothy to apply.

All right, she admitted to herself, *I did more than encourage her.*

Without telling Becca and Ona, she'd contacted Dorothy, owner of the Blithedale Theater, and suggested that Blithedale would benefit if the movie theater thrived. The theater was old-fashioned and poorly attended. Everyone said so. The town needed a cultural hotspot. She was sure Becca and Ona would agree.

But she hadn't asked them before contacting Dorothy. She hadn't mentioned it after she and Dorothy met for coffee at Bonsai & Pie to discuss the matter. Nor after Dorothy called her to accept Alice's invitation to present a revitalization plan to the Future Fund, with the assumption that Alice, Becca, and Ona would support the idea.

The thought of keeping secrets from her new friends made her stomach churn, but, she told herself, she had a good reason to go it alone.

Wonderland Books.

Set in a 400-square foot, log-cabin tiny house on Blithedale's Main Street, Wonderland Books stood on the ground where Alice's mom had once run a bookstore. Before she got cancer and sold the store. Before she died. Before Alice moved in with her aunt and uncle—far from Blithedale.

From the age of 9, she'd felt disconnected from who she really was.

Leaving her fiancé at the altar and fleeing to Blithedale

changed all that, and even though the old bookstore was gone, the Blithedale Future Fund gave her the support to revive it as Wonderland Books.

Let's be honest, she told herself, *Becca and Ona gave me the financial support I needed.*

Her friends had given her a loan on terms that no bank would ever give, drawing on their own funds and additional support from community members to establish the Blithedale Future Fund for the purpose. Ona had built and donated the tiny house. And Alice?

I've done nothing...

Alice grew up self-reliant. She couldn't accept charity forever, even if the fund's support did come in the form of a loan. Becca and Ona meant well. But their help, their generosity—it reminded her of how her fiancé, Rich, had almost suffocated her with his attention.

The memory made her shudder.

No, it's time to stop taking so much—it's time for me to give back.

She only hoped her friends would understand when she revealed her plans tonight.

Besides, it's not like I'm doing this without any guidance.

Next to the box of donated books lay an old, leather-bound notebook. She touched its well-worn cover. It had belonged to Old Mayor Townsend whose statue stood outside the Pemberley Inn, Ona's Jane Austen-inspired boutique hotel, and it contained the old mayor's vision for the town.

Ona gestured toward the book. "Still reading the old mayor's ideas for Blithedale?"

"His ideas are so—so—what's the word...?"

"Outdated?"

"Prescient."

"Fancy word for a lucky guess."

Old Mayor Townsend's vision was anything but a lucky guess. Sure, some ideas wouldn't work today—like his insistence that Main Street should be widened to accommodate a tram—but his basic vision made even more sense in the 21st century: He'd wanted to create a thriving community that offered everything a person might need within walking distance, not least of which was the nature: Blithedale lay nestled in the woods, with the beautiful Hiawatha River splashing lazily through town.

"Blithedale has great potential," Alice said. "Old Mayor Townsend saw that. If we can help fix up some of the rundown buildings and support the struggling businesses…"

"Then we can get a hundred more reviews like this," Ona said.

"Reviews like what?" Becca swept into the bookstore with a Tupperware in her arms and tote bag over her shoulder. "Don't tell me you got a negative customer review."

"Check this out," Ona said as Becca put her Tupperware down on a bench.

Becca Frye owned the What the Dickens Diner, Blithedale's main watering hole, where everyone gathered for meals and gossip. She shook the tote bag off her broad shoulder and a gap-toothed grin spread across her face.

"A review like this would never have appeared in *The Blithedale Record*."

Ona shook her head. "Not in a million years."

The Blithedale Record, the local newspaper, had shut down. After being involved in a scandal that sent his brother to prison, the newspaper's owner and sole journalist, Todd Townsend, had skipped town.

"I do sometimes wonder what happened to him," Alice said.

Ona raised her one visible eyebrow, the other being hidden by her eyepatch. "I hope you're not losing sleep over

Todd Townsend. I'm sure he's halfway across the country, running a new tabloid and spinning lies."

"Or he's learned from his mistakes and he's turned over a new leaf."

"You're an optimist and an angel, Alice," Becca said, smiling at her. "Like your mom was. And maybe you're right. You know what Estella says in *Great Expectations?*"

Alice and Ona exchanged a smile, and they both shook their heads. Becca was always quoting Charles Dickens, her favorite author, and the central theme of her diner.

"She says, 'I have been bent and broken, but—I hope—into a better shape.'"

"You have a Dickens quote for every occasion," Ona said with a laugh.

"And donuts for every occasion, too."

Becca bent over the Tupperware and pulled off its lid. Alice and Ona made ooh sounds. Inside were rows of donuts —powdered, glazed, and jelly-filled. And digging into the tote, Becca produced a thermos and three cups.

"Decaf coffee. You can't talk business without coffee."

She set the three cups on a bookshelf.

Alice eyed them, butterflies fluttering in her stomach. She checked the time on her phone. It was 5:15 pm. She should tell them everything before Dorothy arrived at half past.

"We're going to need a fourth cup," she said.

Becca and Ona looked at her.

"A fourth cup?" Becca said.

"Who else is coming?" Ona said.

Alice took a deep breath. "You know how much the Blithedale Future Fund's support has meant to me. Ona, you gifted me one of your beautiful tiny houses. And with the support of locals, I've been able to stock my bookshop. But if it hadn't been for the fund's financial aid, I would never have been able to afford the property. Without your support, none of this—" She gestured around at the rafters, the bookshelves. "—would exist."

"It's a loan," Ona said with a shrug. "No biggie."

"But it is a big deal. A huge deal. And while I pay back my loan, I also need to pay back in other ways."

"Sweetie," Becca said. "You don't need to pay back anything."

"But I do," Alice insisted. "And I'm starting by helping an important business in Blithedale take a leap forward."

Ona nodded. "Great. That's why we're here, isn't it? To figure out the applications for the next round of support? So we can review applicants and select the next recipient."

"See, the things is…" Alice bit her lip. "I've already identified the next recipient."

"You've done what?"

Becca put a hand on Ona's arm. "Tell us more, Alice. We're listening."

Alice described how she'd studied Old Mayor Townsend's notes on Blithedale's development, and one point he kept coming back to was the idea of investing in the spaces where people congregate.

"He mentions the church. He mentions the eatery, which is where the diner stands today. And he mentions the theater." She tapped the cover of the notebook with a finger. "It's all in here. If we revitalize the theater, it will not only create a hub for entertainment in town, it will also attract people from outside. So that's why I contacted Dorothy Bowers…"

Ona frowned. "You contacted Dorothy?"

"Well, we hadn't announced that the fund was accepting applications, so I got ahead of the game. I called her. I asked her what she'd do if she had funding to revitalize the theater."

"What did she do, yell at you and hang up?"

"She can be a tough cookie," Becca said. "She rubs a lot of people the wrong way."

"She wasn't rude at all," Alice said. "In fact, she got excited. She said she knew exactly what to do, and that she'd present her full plans to us."

"We can always listen to what she has to say," Becca said. "It's not as if we've promised her anything."

"Well…" Alice felt her face grow hot. "I did meet with her for a coffee and kind of encouraged her…"

"I can't believe it," Ona said, arms across her chest, a deep frown on her face.

Alice checked her phone, afraid to look Ona in the eyes. "Dorothy will be here any minute now."

Ona lapsed into silence. Becca unscrewed the thermos top and poured coffee into three cups. She handed one to Ona, one to Alice, and then took one herself.

"Alice," she said. "You should've told us."

"I know, I know, but—"

"Not because Ona and I somehow decide what happens. In fact, we don't want to decide. No, it's because you can't handle the whole thing by yourself. No one can."

"Yeah," Ona said. "It's a lot."

Alice flinched inwardly. *They're my friends,* she reminded herself. But another voice in her weighed in: *So, why don't they think I'm competent enough to handle Dorothy's plans?*

"Let's see what Dorothy says," she mumbled.

Ona and Becca exchanged a look. Then Becca said, "Good idea. Let's see what she says, and then we can take it from there."

Ona sipped her coffee. Becca sat down on one of the small benches next to the bookshelves, and she grabbed a donut and nibbled at its edges. An unusual silence descended on them as they waited, and Alice busied herself with her box of donations.

After she'd opened Wonderland Books, many local citizens had emptied their attics and basements and garages of old paperbacks and hardbacks, eager to help her with stock. Most of the books were junk. Tattered copies of thrillers that no longer sold. Mildew-stained editions of abridged classics. A dozen *Merck Manuals* from 1992.

But occasionally she found treasure.

She laid one such book on the small counter. A first edition of A. A. Milne's *The House at Pooh Corner*. A tear in the dust jacket and a cracked spine were unforgivable sins in the world of pristine, auctionable first editions, but only a handful of pages had stains, and to a genuine lover of the Hundred Acre Wood, this copy would be a delight.

Alice flipped through the book. Usually she would've taken great pleasure in the classic illustrations. But she was too aware of the awkward silence in the bookstore.

Once Dorothy gets here and they see her plans, everything will be all right again.

Further down in the box, she found a badly beat-up first edition of the Nancy Drew book, *Mystery of Crocodile Island*. This one she'd keep for herself. She loved Nancy Drew. In fact, she adored all kinds of books—her childhood favorite was *Alice's Adventures in Wonderland*—but once she'd discovered mysteries as a kid, she'd been smitten. Her mom had solved several mysteries in Blithedale, endearing herself even more to the locals. According to Becca, Alice had the same knack—or compulsion—for putting her nose in police matters.

The last discovery was a beautiful box set of L. Frank Baum's Oz books—all 14 in the series, starting with *The Wonderful Wizard of Oz* and ending with *Glinda of Oz*. It wasn't a first edition, but it would make someone happy—whether that was a collector or a kid.

She sorted through the rest of the books. Some good, mostly bad. And then checked the time again.

"Is Dorothy the punctual type?" she asked.

"Dorothy is—" Ona paused. "—the interesting type."

Her tone of voice suggested that "interesting" was a euphemism.

"Are you telling me she's flakey?"

"Oh, no," Becca said. "Quite the opposite. If Dorothy decides to do something, she's like a bull seeing red. Nothing will stop her."

Alice looked at her watch. "Well, something clearly has. She's late."

Ona shrugged. "Dorothy runs on Dorothy time."

They drank coffee, ate donuts, and waited for their guest of honor, and with every minute that passed, Alice felt more and more uncomfortable. She couldn't help but remember what her friends had said about her not being capable of handling this kind of thing. She needed to prove she could give back to them.

"I'll give Dorothy a call," she said.

But the phone rang and rang, and Dorothy didn't answer.

Finally, Alice put her phone away. She was so ashamed of how this was turning out that she wasn't able to look her friends in the eyes. She hurried out from behind the counter.

"I'll be right back," she said. "I'm going to find Dorothy— you stay here."

Want more? Join Alice and her friends in the next book: *A Theater to Die For*

MORE BY M.P. BLACK

A Wonderland Books Cozy Mystery Series

A Bookshop to Die For

A Theater to Die For

A Halloween to Die For

A Christmas to Die For

An Italian-American Cozy Mystery Series

The Soggy Cannoli Murder

Sambuca, Secrets, and Murder

Tastes Like Murder

Meatballs, Mafia, and Murder

Short stories

The Italian Cream Cake Murder

ABOUT THE AUTHOR

M.P. Black writes fun cozies with an emphasis on food, books, and travel — and, of course, a good old murder mystery.

In addition to writing and publishing his own books, he helps others fulfill their author dreams too.

M.P. Black has lived in many places, including Austria, Costa Rica, and the United Kingdom. Today, he lives in Copenhagen, Denmark, with his family.

Join M.P. Black's free newsletter for updates on books and special deals:

https://mpblackbooks.com/newsletter/

Printed in Great Britain
by Amazon

41852602R00128